C0-AWE-264

Your Murderer

Russian Theatre Archive

A series of books edited by John Freedman (Moscow), Leon Gitelman (St Petersburg) and Anatoly Smeliansky (Moscow)

Volume 1
The Major Plays of Nikolai Erdman
translated and edited by John Freedman

Volume 2
A Meeting About Laughter
Sketches, Interludes and Theatrical Parodies by Nikolai Erdman
with Vladimir Mass and Others
translated and edited by John Freedman

Volume 3
Theatre in the Solovki Prison Camp
Natalia Kuziakina

Volume 4
Sergei Radlov: The Shakespearian Fate of a Soviet Director
David Zolotnitsky

Volume 5
Bulgakov: The Novelist–Playwright
edited by Lesley Milne

Volume 6
Aleksandr Vampilov: The Major Plays
translated and edited by Alma Law

Volume 7
The Death of Tarelkin and Other Plays:
The Trilogy of Alexander Sukhovo-Kobylin
translated and edited by Harold B. Segel

Volume 8
A Chekhov Quartet
translated and adapted by Vera Gottlieb

Volume 9
Two Plays from the New Russia
Bald/Brunet by Daniil Gink and *Nijinsky* by Alexei Burykin
translated and edited by John Freedman

Volume 10
Russian Comedy of the Nikolaian Era
translated and with an introduction by Laurence Senelick

Volume 11
Meyerhold Speaks / Meyerhold Rehearses
by Aleksandr Gladkov
translated, edited and with an introduction by Alma Law

Please see the back of this book for other titles in the Russian Theatre Archive series

Your Murderer

by Vassily Aksyonov

translated by Daniel Gerould
and Jadwiga Kosicka
with and introduction
by Daniel Gerould

harwood academic publishers

Australia • Canada • France • Germany • India
Japan • Luxembourg • Malaysia • The Netherlands
Russia • Singapore • Switzerland

 Printed in Singapore.

Amsteldijk 166
1st Floor
1079 LH Amsterdam
The Netherlands

British Library Cataloguing in Publication Data
Aksyonov, Vassily
Your murderer. - (Russian theatre archive; v. 18)
1. Satire - Drama
I. Title II. Gerould, Daniel, 1928 –
891.7'2'44

ISBN 90-5755-103-9

CONTENTS

INTRODUCTION TO THE SERIES

The Russian Theatre Archive makes available in English the best avant-garde plays from the pre-Revolutionary period to the present day. It features monographs on major playwrights and theatre directors, introductions to previously unknown works, and studies of the main artistic groups and periods.

Plays are presented in performing edition translations, including (where appropriate) musical scores, and instructions for music and dance. Whenever possible the translated texts will be accompanied by videotapes of performances of plays in the original language.

PREFACE

I could write a new play about the story of my play *Your Murderer*, which, I must confess, has never been staged. The genesis of the play goes back to time immemorial – 1963. At that point our gang of young Soviet writers were licking the wounds inflicted during the Kremlin meeting with the leaders of the Communist party. We felt humiliated by Khrushschev's assault on post-Stalinist literature. How did an ignorant Bolshevik dare to teach us how to write and threaten to wipe us off the face of the earth if we didn't comply with his demands? On the other hand, many of the whipping boys, myself included, blamed themselves for their lack of courage, for their shameful silence in the face of a hostile audience and, to some degree, for selling out our newly acquired principles of artistic freedom. *Your Murderer* was written in the wake of that Kremlin meeting and it reflects those sentiments and the artists' decision to resist. In a way it belonged to a genre well known in Russia since the time of Lermontov, named after his poem *The Turk's Complaints*: it had a fictitious setting, fictitious protagonists, but the grievances were real.

I hadn't the slightest hope of having my play staged when, out of the blue, I got an offer from Anatoly Efros, then artistic director of the Lenkom Theatre. "It is a very topical play," he said, "we need to show that the artist is not supposed to sell out his art." I was delighted: it was a big deal at that time to be staged by the outstanding director of such a famous playhouse. Sad to say, shortly after that Mr. Efros was criticized by the Moscow party committee for the way he ran his theatre and was ousted from his position.

The second attempt to stage *Your Murderer* took place twenty years later in the United States when director Paul Berman staged a public reading of the play at the George Street Theatre in Brunswick, New Jersey. It was a success with an audience of the theatre's patrons. To my total surprise, the play seemed not to have lost its topicality. What surprised me even more was the reaction to this success on the part of the George Street Theatre's artistic director, whose name unfortunately escapes me. He told me confidentially: "Forget about Berman. The play will be staged by me. Or by nobody else." In other words, the self-appointed director wanted the author of *Your Murderer* to resemble the main character of the play with his propensity for selling out people and ideas. My answer to this offer was negative.

In general, I haven't been too lucky with my theatre, although several of my five plays have been brilliantly staged in Moscow, Paris and Belgrade. As far as *Your Murderer*'s vitality is concerned – strange though this may seem, it hasn't lost a scintilla of its topicality, not least in Russia where party and KGB crooks have with great rapidity turned into dubious free-market operators.

Vassily Aksyonov

INTRODUCTION

Although in both Russia and the West he is much better known as a novelist (*The Burn, Quest for an Island, Generations of Winter*) than as a playwright, Vassily Aksyonov before his forced emigration from the USSR in 1981 wrote five unusual plays that challenged the reigning norms of Soviet theatre and proposed a radically different model. The first four – *Always on Sale* (1963), *Your Murderer* (1964), *The Four Temperaments* (1967), and *Aristophaniana and the Frogs* (1967–68) – were all composed in Moscow as the state began its first serious crackdown on artistic freedom of expression since the Thaw. None of Aksyonov's plays could be published in the Soviet Union, and only one was actually staged: *Always on Sale* in 1965 at Moscow's Sovremennik (Contemporary) Theatre in a splendidly combative production by the theatre's managing director, Oleg Efremov. Even though highly popular with audiences, Aksyonov's theatrical debut was kept carefully under wraps by the authorities who allowed the rambunctious and subversive comedy to be played only rarely and exclusively in Moscow – a typical Soviet brand of oblique censorship that sought to reduce the number of spectators exposed to the infection of dangerous ideas.

I remember that when I was in Moscow in 1967 on an exchange program, I tried in vain to get a ticket to what was perhaps one of only two or three performances of *Always on Sale* for the entire season (in this case playing not at the Sovremennik itself, but in another venue as a guest appearance). With nowhere else to turn, I appealed to Aksyonov, with whom I had recently become acquainted, but even he was unable to make any headway with the box office or theatre management. There simply were no tickets to be had for the totally sold-out performance. The resourceful author found another way to solve the problem – on the evening of the performance he met me at the theatre a few minutes before curtain time and escorted me, past deferential and admiring ticket-takers, into the auditorium. I eventually got a place – a "strapontin," one of those folding seats attached to aisle chairs that are used for overflow audiences. The playwright had to stand at the back of the auditorium for the more than two hours that the show lasted, but like everyone else there he seemed elated by the truculent high spirits of the acting and staging.

Both play and performance transported spectators away from the somber banalities of contemporary Soviet drama and back to the great Russian tradition of grotesque satire represented by Sukhovo-Kobylin's *Death of Tarelkin* and Mayakovsky's *Bedbug*, both then playing in Moscow (although the former lasted only a week before being taken off for its too vivid portrayal of police state interrogation techniques). The kinship of style and sensibility between these plays and *Always on Sale* was striking and by no means accidental. I shall return to this theme a little later, but first I must complete the survey of Aksyonov's unnaturally brief career as a playwright.

Barred from having his plays published or performed, Aksyonov gave up the stage. It was only a decade later in 1979 that he wrote his final theatrical work, *The Heron*, shortly after he had circulated his unauthorized and uncensored literary almanach *Metropol* in an edition of a dozen copies – an act of defiance that forced him out of the Soviet Union and into emigration to the United States. The author subsequently explained: "I wrote this play in the winter of 1979, sitting in my own dacha, in Peredelkino, a writers' village near Moscow, having already been ousted from the Writers' Union and all official Soviet literature. . . . I didn't expect it to be staged at all, so I wrote a lot of very extended stage directions there, and some verses too. I adapted it for reading, because I didn't expect any changes in the attitude toward me. I couldn't imagine that this play would be suitable for the Soviet theatre at all."

Like all the author's theatrical works, *The Heron* overstepped boundaries and crossed genres. Convinced of the impossibility of ever having his work staged, Aksyonov wrote a play that stretched the limits of dramatic form by combining short prose poems and lengthy stage directions with dialogue. By the time *The Heron* was given its premiere in 1984 – in Paris directed by Antoine Vitez (a fellow Russian by origin) – the author was already in exile.

Soviet censorship and state repression succeeded in cutting short what should have been a brilliant career as a playwright. Yet even so the five plays that Aksyonov did write were the most formally innovative of the period, breaking totally with the imposed codes of socialist realism and re-establishing continuity with the great Russian tradition of fantastic satire and avant-garde experimentation of the 1920s.

Before turning to *Your Murderer*, I should say a few words about Aksyonov's theatrical debut with *Always on Sale* and the circumstances surrounding it. In the early 1960s, Aksyonov was celebrated for his innovative stories and novels such as *Colleagues*, *Halfway to the Moon*, and *A Ticket to the Stars* that dealt with the new, post-war generation of Soviet youth. Attacked by establishment critics as morally and aesthetically unsound, these books quickly became popular with readers in Russia and were translated and acclaimed throughout the world.

Both in form and content Aksyonov's fiction was unorthodox. His heroes spoke a colloquial language full of juicy slang, copied Western taste in dress and music, and traveled light without cumbersome ideological baggage.

Skeptical, yet naive, these uncommitted young people were in quest of romance and fellowship, hoping to fill the void in their empty personal lives and satisfy their vague yearnings for the heroic and meaningful.

Since Aksyonov – himself only thirty in 1962 – depicted his characters sympathetically and honestly, he became something of a spokesman for the new generation as well as a leader of the emerging group of young Soviet writers associated with it. By the mid-1960s, however, Aksyonov abandoned the youth theme and turned his attention to artistic problems, attempting through stylistic experimentation and verbal parody to recapture the linguistic vitality and technical virtuosity of the early Soviet avant-garde. He was fascinated by the absurdist experiments of Daniil Kharms, Aleksandr Vvedensky, and the OBERIU group that had been forcibly suppressed in the 1930s.

To rehabilitate and reanimate a silenced tradition Aksyonov the novelist turned to the theatre in the mid-1960s and began writing grotesque satires for the stage. As a playwright, Aksyonov performed an invaluable service: he reestablished contact between modern Soviet drama and the great line of Russian and early Soviet satirists, starting with Gogol, Sukhovo-Kobylin, and Saltykov-Shchedrin and continuing through Mayakovsky, Erdman and Bulgakov (all of whom were victims of state oppression).

Aksyonov approached the theatre not as a novelist working in an unfamiliar idiom, but as a natural playwright gifted with a powerful scenic imagination. Bold images, striking gestures, and a montage of sound became the writer's new-found means of expression in *Always on Sale*, enabling him to transcend the purely literary. The resulting multi-layered theatrical text called for the use of mask, chant, song and dance, non-realistic lighting and skeletal setting, all elements of staging that Efremov employed to great effect in the production at the Contemporary Theatre.

In *Always on Sale* Aksyonov strips away the facade of a Moscow apartment house to reveal the lives of a tragicomic cross-section of the inhabitants of the Soviet capital. In an expressionistic fashion the characters' inner longings and nightmarish dreams continually burst through the surface of drab everyday reality. The idealistic but boring and ineffectual do-gooder Treugolnikov is pitted against the charismatic rogue Kistochkin, a cynical and opportunistic journalist making his way to the top as the Soviet new man. Played with diabolical verve by Mikhail Kozakov, the satanic anti-hero, whose honesty, honor, friendship, and love is "always on sale," is a modern and more insidious version of Mayakovsky's parasite Prysipkin in *The Bedbug*. Kistochkin has an important ally in the salesperson of the neighborhood kiosk (serving in the Russia of those days as a combination snack bar, variety store, and pharmacy). This malevolent choral figure and fury (played by Oleg Tabakov) presides as the reigning deity of the play, gleefully informing customers that she is out of whatever they request. In his egotistical fantasies,

Kistochkin projects a totalitarian society over which he rules as dictator, while Treugolnikov dreams of a world of harmony, love, and mutual respect. In an Aristophanic epilogue in which all wishes are fulfilled in defiance of reality, Kistochkin himself becomes transformed into the kiosk-lady who now politely fills all orders and announces that everything is "always on sale."

After seeing the production, I wanted to read the play and I remember one morning asking Aksyonov if he could lend me a copy of *Always on Sale*. The previous evening we lost track of time talking and drinking and I had stayed over at his apartment rather than try to get back to my room at Moscow State University. The author rummaged around in huge piles of notebooks and papers to no avail. Failing to find his first play, he gave me a copy of his second, *Your Murderer,* "An Anti-Alcoholic Comedy in Eight Scenes with a Prologue and an Epilogue," neatly typed on 94 sheets of yellow paper. As I left, I promised to return the play. Aksyonov said I need not bother, which I interpreted as meaning for me to take *Your Murderer* back to America and do with it as I saw fit. When it could no longer harm the author, I published a translation. I should point out that the revised Russian text of the play that Aksyonov published in his collected plays in 1981 after his emigration is called *Kiss, Orchestra, Fish, Sausage*. Now and then it differs very slightly in phrasing from *Your Murderer,* but is identical in all significant ways. This translation follows Aksyonov's original text.

Your Murderer takes over theme and structure from *Always on Sale*. Both plays feature grotesque metamorphosis, accelerating demagoguery that produces craven conformity, deepening nightmare followed by an ironically triumphant epilogue, and mirror-image opposition between a prissy, well-intentioned humanist and a raunchy, foul-mouthed but engaging conman. And in both cases these satirical techniques serve the didactic purpose of exploring rival concepts of true and false community.

But although *Your Murderer* retains the dialectical structure of idealistic hero and seductive anti-hero battling for control of "reality," the formula is now applied to "the eternal theme of the artist and power," which has become the author's major concern since the state clamped down on the arts shortly after the composition of *Always on Sale*. As Aksyonov later explained, "The play was written under the influence of the ideas expounded at the historic meeting of the Party and Government leaders with representatives of the creative intelligentsia in March 1963 in the Kremlin. Funny as it may seem, the play was being prepared for production at Moscow's Lenin Komsomol Theatre. Alas, managing director Efros angered the mighty comrade Egorychev, and therefore it would have been possible to dedicate the play to that comrade, then living in Copenhagen as an ambassador of the USSR."

Here Aksyonov is referring to the meetings of March 7 and 8 at which Nikita Khrushchev denounced a number of young writers for pursuing the "rotten idea of absolute freedom" instead of communist partisanship, accusing them of abstractionism, formalism and other bourgeois distortions. Aksyonov and the poet Andrei Voznesensky were pressured to apologize for an interview they had given in Moscow to the Polish journal *Polityka* at which they had declared their intention to bypass the generation of the fathers (the current stagnant communist leadership) in order to return to the earlier tradition of the grandfathers (the true revolutionary spirit). Their recantations were clearly ironic and double-edged; Aksyonov declared in *Pravda* of April 3 that he was trying to create his own positive hero.

The starting point of *Your Murderer* is the threat to the arts in the Soviet Union after the meeting between Khrushchev and the artistic intelligentsia. The playwright evokes the period through the use of Soviet media clichés and provides many echoes of the techniques of repression then being applied. For example, toward the end of Scene II in which the police come to evict Alexandro from his hovel, the dialogue between the writer and the police repeats almost verbatim the transcript of Joseph Brodsky's examination by the judge during his trial in March 1964 when the twenty-three-year-old poet was condemned as a social parasite and banished to a work camp in Siberia.

In this respect *Your Murderer* is very much a play of its time, directly reflecting the plight of Soviet artists in the 1960s and the cultural politics of the cold war. But by abandoning the "real" Moscow setting of *Always on Sale* and casting his second play in the form of a parable about life on a blessed isle, Aksyonov makes his "Anti-Alcoholic Comedy" part of a utopian and anti-utopian literary tradition that is of universal application and open to diverse interpretations.

The idea of an island free of oppression has its origins in More's *Utopia* and Bacon's *New Atlantis*. In Russian literature the island theme has a history going back to the Decembrist poets Kondraty Ryleev and Aleksandr Bestuzhev who wrote a poem in praise of liberty entitled "The Islands." In the 1920s and '30s the device was used for satirical purposes in Mikhail Bulgakov's *Crimson Island* and Ilf and Petrov's *Island of Peace*. Aksyonov carries on this tradition, linking the dream of freedom to art and combining Pushkin's idea of a remote asylum where the poet can find peace with Bulgakov's notion of a sanctuary as the posthumous reward for persecution and suffering.

In *Your Murderer* the two realities confronting one another occupy different spaces: free creativity on the island and vigilant control in the city. When they go from the island to the city, the small band of struggling artists are exterminated by totalitarian power, but later resurrected to lead productive lives in the paradisal utopia on the Edenic island where they started their journey.

In all his satirical works Aksyonov functions as a moralist exposing human venality and folly. In *Your Murderer* the playwright extends his ironic scrutiny to the artist and his role in society, demonstrating that when false community seduces creativity the noble-minded intellectual can produce the worst monsters. The pious writer–hero of *Your Murderer* actually fathers Pork Sausage, the cynical, bawdy anti-hero who presides, as lord of misrule, over a corrupt commonwealth and its perverted revels. Structurally, Aksyonov centers the climax of *Your Murderer* on recognition of the close blood relationship between fatuously high principles and ludicrously low realities, and he underscores the point through the device of ironic citation, which is characteristic of the entire work with its many intertextual cultural references.

Twice Alexandro, hoping to erase the effects of his creative complicity by destroying his child, threatens Pork Sausage, "I fathered you, and I killed you." In Nikolai Gogol's famous historical romance *Taras Bulba*, the Cossack warrior chieftain uses the exact same words when he kills his son Andrei for deserting to the enemy because of a woman. In Aksyonov's play, it is ultimately the treacherous son Pork Sausage, who, in an ironic inversion, reverses the formula for the third and final time ("You fathered me"), as he prepares to destroy his creator. The artist's creative imagination, once it has gone awry, proves to be its own deadliest enemy; you yourself are "Your Murderer," as the title of the play suggests. Pork Sausage also resembles the nose in Gogol's tale of the same name, which once severed from its owner's face acquires a life of its own.

Presenting an allusive story in universal terms that are open to varying interpretations, the parable play can serve as an analogue to many different social situations. The central metaphor of *Your Murderer* – the Masculinus Company as a ubiquitous, all-powerful cartel that engulfs the world and swallows up those most opposed to it – cuts in several directions. Audiences living under totalitarian systems know how to "read" the signs in contradictory fashions. The allusive Aesopian parable is an instrument upon which Aksyonov plays with virtuosity, making what appears to be officially acceptable anti-capitalist satire actually applicable in every particular to the contemporary Soviet regime. References in the play to "forbidden" Russians point to the true revolutionaries of the early years, not to the contemporary party hacks who maintain the status quo in order to stay in power.

Armed with the technological power of modern media, the Company's only ideology is its own continued operation and self-perpetuation. With Mayakovsky Aksyonov shares a fascination with the gadgets and machinery of the future; in *Your Murderer* these tools are all in the wrong hands. Unlike the bumbling bureaucrats satirized by Mayakovsky in *The Bathhouse,* the Masculinus Company is thorough, efficient, and superficially friendly and benevolent. The Company – or, in other words, the system – works because it engages the best minds. By alternating threats and rewards, the authorities strive to convince the intelligentsia, particularly the artist–intellectual, that it is in one's own self-interest to become a part of the system.

In calling the company Masculinus, Aksyonov stresses the patriarchal nature of a system characterized by machismo. But although Masculinus is male-dominated, paternalistic, and gerontological, disseminating its authoritarian principles from on high, the young are quickly absorbed into the company and women are recruited into sister branches. The company's ambitions are global and all-inclusive. Only five-year-old children dare to make the obvious truth known, by writing everywhere, "Masculinus Destroys Your Health."

At first Alexandro naively attempts to build a utopia in the shadow of the corrupt city, hoping to rediscover the ideals of freedom and creativity that have been lost to dehumanizing jargon in language, thought, and feeling. The writer of fiction thinks love and community can be recovered in simplicity and deprivation; the Masculinus Company, on the contrary, expects to gain allegiance by satisfying ever-expanding material needs. The Freedom Tree – a living, growing presence – is opposed to the Masculinus bottle, a sterile, synthetic, yet addictive product of advertising.

In *Your Murderer* Aksyonov experiments with dramaturgical technique, as he already had explored narrative technique in his stories and novels. The drama being enacted is the invention of its principal character, the novelist Alexandro. The Tree is a product of his art, but then so is the bottle. Duped by his own powers – which prove to be as destructive as they are creative – the artist cannot control the interplay between the real and the imagined. Alexandro chooses to believe in the illusion of the Freedom Tree, while refusing to accept that his cartoon-creation, Pork Sausage, could actually come to life.

The heightened metatheatricality of *Your Murderer* enables Aksyonov to pose the following question: if Alexandro, as author of the play in which he appears, has created the nightmare that engulfs him, could he uncreate it? Perhaps it is only because of the complicity of the intellectual and artistic elite that the system is able to project its images everywhere and triumph. Justifying their complicity by imagining that they are not really serving the system but undermining it, Alexandro and his fellow artists have greater potential for evil than average citizens, like Feodoro, who mindlessly do their menial jobs. Self-deluded by their own creative powers, the poets, painters, and musicians construct imaginative worlds, closing their eyes to actual consequences, and then they are appalled when the results of their acquiescence materialize before them.

Essentially good-hearted but always willing to compromise in order to save his own skin, Feodoro is the everyman of the dangerous concentration-camp world of *Your Murderer*. Devoid of imagination and not subject to the complex self-deceptions of the artist–intellectuals, the practical Feodoro remains close to "reality," however grim it may be. He would like to help Alexandro and immediately warns him of the dangers of serving Masculinus. He offers the novelist a part of his cigarette and is willing to put in a good word for him with the authorities, but as a simple functionary, he must perform his routine duties. When executions take place, Feodoro the accountant records in his ledger the names of those slaughtered. Having lost their youth and ideals, the artist–intellectuals go passively to their death and destruction, victims of their own bad dreams. Feodoro is the survivor.

Like *Always on Sale, Your Murderer* is a synthesis of diverse elements: native Russian traditions of the grotesque, avant-garde tendencies from Soviet satire in the 1920s, and recent developments in Western European drama since the end of World War II. Abandoning the observed milieu and particularized Russian social types of *Always on Sale,* Aksyonov found the appropriate dramatic form for *Your Murderer* in the parable play, a genre that, under the impact of Brecht's late works, flourished particularly in the German-speaking theatre of the 1950s and became well known through dramas such as Dürrenmatt's *The Visit* and Frisch's *The Firebugs,* as well as Ionesco's absurdist fable, *Rhinoceros.*

Aksyonov had a superb model for parable drama close at hand in the fairy tales of Evgenii Shvarts, and *Your Murderer* shows a number of interesting affinities to Shvarts's plays. Like Lancelot, the hero of *The Dragon,* Alexandro is a Don Quixote battling a many-headed monster, and his antagonist, Pork Sausage, further resembles the Dragon in being utterly friendly and familiar, a perfect embodiment of the banality of evil. In its multiple deceptions and macabre transformations, the world of *Your Murderer* recalls the sinister realm of *The Shadow.* Like the scholar hero in that darkest of all Shvarts's fables, Alexandro has a sinister alter ego or double who threatens him with ruin. The true horror lies, not outside the hero, but deep within.

Along with the traditions of Shvarts and the fairy-tale (with its use of beast-masks and animal fable), popular song and dance, jazz, film, and television are all assimilated into Aksyonov's highly original collage. Musical citations range from a George Gershwin song and Aleksandr Vertinsky's famous romance, *Yellow Angel,* to lines quoted by Miquelo and Gregoro, about renouncing the old world and shaking the dust from their feet, which come from *The Workers' Marseillaise,* one of many proletarian versions of the French anthem. From Chaplin's *The Gold Rush,* Alexandro has taken the idea of boiling and eating the soles of his shoes. Juxtaposed to these scraps of popular culture are the deeply emotional love lyrics, recited by Alexandro and Maria, of five great Russian poets, all of whom – starting with Pushkin, who was twice banished for revolutionary sentiments – experienced difficulties with the state because of creative non-conformity. Aksyonov makes the true Russian spirit of revolutionary creativity something dangerous and forbidden in the Masculinus world of bureaucratic regimentation.

Stylistically, *Your Murderer* is a richly grotesque hodgepodge of different linguistic levels. Aksyonov defies all the rules and mixes a powerful cocktail out of traditional Russian proverbs and folk sayings, contemporary slang, bureaucratic jargon and party slogans, invented obscenities, foreign words and phrases (mainly Spanish and English), terminology from sports and heavy drinking, and pure nonsense. Aksyonov's "anti-alcoholic comedy" has a hoary ancestor in allegorical temperance dramas like Tolstoi's *The First Distiller* and the Soviet children's play *Four Million Authors* by Aleksandra Brushtein and Boris Zon in which "Drunkenness is defeated as a huge bottle of vodka is knocked over by two boxers" – with this difference that Aksyonov's characters do not knock the bottle over, but climb into it (a Russian proverbial idiom meaning "to get drunk" that Aksyonov has made literal and visual). *Your Murderer* trenchantly satirizes Russia's "drinking culture," and Masculinus can be read as an allusion to the former Soviet government's very profitable liquor monopoly. The play also prophetically portrays the domination of life by television (and television personalities).

By assimilating such diverse traditions and styles, Aksyonov bursts open the predictable monotony of Soviet drama with its linear story line, uplifting message, and clichéd style. What emerges instead is *Your Murderer*, a modern pop-art parable, multi-layered and rich in associations.

* * *

This version of *Your Murderer* is based on an earlier version published in *Performing Arts Journal*, Vol. 2, No. 1 (Spring 1977).

The Russian poetry of Pasternak, Blok, Mayakovsky, Akhmatova, and Pushkin has been translated by Daniel Gerould.

Your Murderer

An Anti-Alcoholic Comedy in Eight Scenes
With a Prologue and an Epilogue

CHARACTERS

ALEXANDRO,
a writer
MARIA,
his fiancee
MIQUELO,
a painter
GREGORO,
a composer
FEODORO,
a radical liberal or liberal radical
PORK SAUSAGE,
the idol of the nation
SANDWICH MEN (1, 2, and 3),
they are also STOCKHOLDERS Holding a Controlling Share
as well as policemen and attendants
MAN OF INDEPENDENT MEANS
PLAYBOY
ANNOUNCER
BOBO
LOLA
CHIQUITO
BLUE COLLAR WORKER
WHITE COLLAR WORKER
GENERAL

The action takes place in our times in one of the tropical countries of the New World. This country and its nation were only established at the turn of the last century and perhaps due to this fact some kind of confusion still prevails as well as certain tendencies toward banditry, swindling, corruption and alcoholism. But the main cause of all these nasty things is, needless to say, the capitalist system with its fierce and ruthless battles among monopolies.

SCENE ONE

(The rear of the stage presents a contemporary earthly "paradise:" an endless line of dazzlingly golden beaches and equally dazzling white skyscrapers, a bright shining blue sky with advertising sausages and balloons floating across it.

At the front of the stage – the trunk of a palm tree. Alexandro sits perched in the palm. Below under the palm Maria, Miquelo and Gregoro are on their knees looking up at Alexandro.)

MARIA: Are you shaking it?
ALEXANDRO: Yes, of course, I'm shaking it. Can't you see I am?
MIQUELO: (*Naively.*) But why doesn't anything fall down?
MARIA: Because he's doing a lousy job of shaking.
GREGORO: (*Good-hearted.*) No, he's not doing such a lousy job of shaking.
MARIA: If you ask me, he's not shaking at all. He's been brooding about what's going to happen to us! He's a maniac, that's what he is!
MIQUELO: Hey, Alexandro, shake it a little harder!
GREGORO: Yesterday he shook it a bit more energetically!
MARIA: He sure did! Yesterday we still had something to eat. Alex! If you want me to love you, shake it like a man!

(*Alexandro shakes the palm tree with redoubled force, but unfortunately nothing falls down.*)

ALEXANDRO: Hey, friends, hey, Maria, congratulate me! I just thought up a brilliant denouement. The forces of evil will be driven back and crushed. Listen, you guys, I am a genius! No doubt about it. You'll be totally delighted with what's going to happen to you. Everything will be absolutely marvelous.
MIQUELO: Who can last till the denouement on an empty stomach!
GREGORO: It's a waste of breath even talking about it.
MARIA: That crazy writer is planning to starve us to death. He's going to send his friends to kingdom come, and drive his beloved into the grave. The tyrant!

(The noise of an approaching helicopter can be heard.)

MIQUELO: That helicopter's coming by again.
GREGORO: *(Looking up.)* It's the advertising helicopter for the Masculinus Company again. Look at that huge bottle it's pulling!
MIQUELO: I wonder who designs those labels for them? I'd say he's a good artist.
GREGORO: You'd have done a better job, old boy.

(The noise of the helicopter's motor grows louder and louder. A song amplified through a loud-speaker drifts down from the helicopter.)

Masculinus!
Masculinus!
Won't you cheer us!
Won't you cheer us!
Throughout the world both son and dad
To drink whisky would be glad
Masculinus!

MARIA: What wouldn't I give for a glass of Masculinus right now. Oh, I'm sick and tired of being poor!
GREGORO: What a primitive tune! I'd have written a better one for them.
MIQUELO: Of course, you'd have written a better one, after all you're ...

(The noise of the motor drowns out his words.)

POWERFUL VOICE FROM THE HELICOPTER: Greetings! Greetings! The Masculinus Company greets the entire adult population of this great country of ours! We take pleasure in informing you that starting today ten additional Masculinus bars will be opened along the shore. If due to illness or advanced age you are unable to visit your local Masculinus bar, our boys will be glad to serve you at home. Dial zero, zero, zero, zero, zero, zero, zero, zero. Drink Masculinus whisky!

Masculinus!
Masculinus!
Won't you cheer us!
Won't you cheer us!
Throughout the world both son and dad
To drink whisky would be glad
Masculinus!

(The noise fades out. The helicopter flies off. The huge letters MASCULINUS appear for a moment in the distance above the skyscrapers.)

GREGORO: If I could just get my hands on a ten-spot, I'd buy a whole bottle of Masculinus.
MIQUELO: I'd give my best painting for a bottle of Masculinus. I'd drink it down in one long gulp.
MARIA: And what about you, Alexandro?
ALEXANDRO: (*From the palm tree*) You've all gone crazy over that Masculinus. It isn't part of the plot. I'm totally satisfied with coconut milk. It's a pure product, uncontaminated by any advertising gimmicks.
MARIA: (*Venomously.*) Are you totally satisfied with tearing holes in your only pair of trousers on that palm tree?
ALEXANDRO: I'm absolutely free here!
MARIA: Then shake it!
MIQUELO AND GREGORO: Shake it, Alexandro! We're hungry!

(*Enter* Feodoro. *He is smoking.*)

FEODORO: Still in the same position? So even that heroic knight, Señor Alexandro, is still sitting perched in the same position in the palm tree? Ciao, friends!

(*They all greet him with a loud "Ciao."*)

GREGORO: (*With a hungry gleam in his eyes.*) You wouldn't happen to have a cigarette, would you, Feodoro?
FEODORO: (*Absentmindedly goes through all his pockets*) I forgot to buy any.
GREGORO: Maybe you wouldn't mind giving me a puff?

(Feodoro *gives him the butt.* Gregoro *inhales greedily.*)

MIQUELO: Leave me some. Leave me a fair share.
MARIA: Would you believe it, Feodoro, that man has been sitting there all day long in that palm tree, and he doesn't have a single thing to show for it. He's completely forgotten how to shake it.
FEODORO: No results at all?
MARIA: None at all, sad to say.
FEODORO: What about yesterday?
MARIA: Only two miserable coconuts. Hardly enough for breakfast and brushing one's teeth.
MIQUELO: (*To* Gregoro.) You promised to give me that butt.
GREGORO: (*Smokes greedily.*) Have a little patience, Miquelo.
MIQUELO: (*Indignantly.*) You're already smoking the trademark.
GREGORO: What are you talking about, there are a good three millimeters to the trademark.
FEODORO: (*Sorrowfully watching the argument between* Gregoro *and* Miquelo.) Alexandro, you can see for yourself what that raving of yours about the Freedom Tree has led to. It's all utter rubbish.

ALEXANDRO: (*Jumps down from the palm tree*) But you don't realize how creative we've become. Feodoro, if you only knew how creative we've become here under the Freedom Tree! Move to one side, you representative of vanity, stand over there! We'll show you. (Alexandro *sits down at the foot of the palm tree with his back against the trunk and begins to speak in a low tone of voice.*) Guys, our time has come: Gregoro, Miquelo, Maria cast off your discontent and be exactly what you are, free under the Freedom Tree. (*At these words the light on the stage changes: the bright, sparkling light is replaced by a golden-green evening and the skyscrapers in the distance merge into a dark broken line resembling a mountain range. The palm tree starts a quiet, slow rotation.* Gregoro, Maria *and* Miquelo *draw near the proscenium. They have a look of reflective concentration.* Feodoro *stands to one side and views the proceedings with astonishment*)

ALEXANDRO: Begin, Gregoro! Forget about our hunger and about Masculinus whisky, forget about the struggle between the avant-gardists and the traditionalists! Go ahead, old boy, create the true and the beautiful!

(Gregoro *stands motionless as if he were listening to something. Music floats down from nowhere.* Gregoro *starts composing.*)

ALEXANDRO: Dance, Maria! Dance, my darling! Don't think about those rich old goats who want to seduce you by honking the horns on their Jaguars! You are my beloved under the Freedom Tree! Create the true and the beautiful!

(Maria *starts to dance. Her dance – resembling neither classical ballet nor stage show – is a spontaneous improvisation to* Gregoro*'s music.*)

ALEXANDRO: Miquelo, get rid of that cigarette butt. Create the true and the beautiful! You are a great artist, the whole sky can serve as your canvas. Forget all our misfortunes and the directives from the Department of Social Harmony! Go, work!

(Miquelo *throws away the cigarette butt and moves confidently towards the back of the stage, to the backdrop. He covers it with broad, bright strokes of color. [It should be obvious that this whole scene must be treated somewhat humorously by means of* Alexandro*'s intonations, the movements of his friends, and all other possible means.]*)

ALEXANDRO: (*To Feodoro.*) Now do you see how we work here, how we create the true and the beautiful?

FEODORO: And what do you do?

ALEXANDRO: How do you like that? What do I do? *I* create. You see, we're all under the Freedom Tree: Gregoro, Miquelo and Maria, they all create – which means I create. And you've come to us with your rationalistic advice. That's my creation too.

FEODORO: It's immoral to transform one's friends into fictional characters.

ALEXANDRO: On the contrary. I transform fictional characters into my friends, I give them shape and substance, I even sleep with Maria. Believe me, old pal, I love her a great deal. And then I'm obliged to feed them. That's why I spend long hours up in that palm tree. There's no time even for writing.

FEODORO: But are they satisfied?

ALEXANDRO: You bet they are. After all, we're absolutely free here. Luxury cruisers don't come near our sandy beaches, and yachts loaded with rampaging tourists pass by at safe distance. We're far removed from your worldly preoccupations. We create – and that's all we do. You're the only one who comes to visit us, and twice a day the Masculinus Company advertising helicopter flies overhead. Believe me, I had a hard time dragging Maria and friends here, but now they're absolutely satisfied . .

FEODORO: So in general your narrative is developing without a hitch, is that right?

ALEXANDRO: (*Proudly.*) That's right!

FEODORO: Something totally idyllic, no friction, no conflicts, is that right?

ALEXANDRO: (*Laughing.*) Of course not. We're sick and tired of your friction, we've had it up to here with your conflicts. (*In a quiet, serious tone of voice*) Thank you very much, we've suffered more than enough in those cities of yours. (*Joyfully once again.*) The only thing is, you're seducing my heroes with your cigarettes, and then there's that idiotic helicopter making us thirsty. Mephistopheles!

FEODORO: But you're having some trouble with food, aren't you?

ALEXANDRO: Just temporary trouble. I'll just shake that palm tree … (*Gets up.*)

(*Bright daylight breaks through. The palm tree stops rotating, the previous scene comes back again.* Miquelo, Maria *and* Feodoro *come over to* Alexandro.)

MARIA: (*With her hands on her hips.*) Say, what's going on, honey? When are we going to eat?

GREGORO: Maybe you should shake it some more, Alexandro?

MIQUELO: That's right, old boy, fairy tales won't feed nightingales.

FEODORO: I wouldn't mind something to nibble on either. There'd be nothing wrong with offering a guest a bite.

ALEXANDRO: (*Cheerfully*) Why, all right, coming up! (*Climbs the palm tree, shakes it.*)

(*From above a human* Head *falls to the stage with a dull thud. It rolls a bit. Then it stops. In utter astonishment all the characters observe this unexpected phenomenon.*)

ALEXANDRO: (*Jumps down from the palm tree, brushes off his hands.*) Nothing to it once you get the hang. (*Notices the* Head.) And just what is this?

HEAD: Life itself. An intrusion by life in all its brutality.

ALEXANDRO: That isn't a part of the plot. I never even thought of tricks

like that. Even in my subconscious there was never anything like that.
HEAD: How do you know, buddy? Step aside, buddy!

(*Thoroughly disconcerted,* Alexandro *steps aside.*)

HEAD: (*Rolls its eyes and sticks out its tongue, babbles idly and frivolously.*) Buenos tardes, Guten Tag, Bonjour, Zdrastvuyte! The Advertising Department of the Masculinus Company greets our dear hermits. Well now, kiddies, how is life treating you? What are your goals and aspirations?
ALEXANDRO: (*Gazing at the* Head, *lost in thought*) Why are those sickening features so familiar to me?
MARIA: (*Comes over to the* Head *swinging her hips*) The day before yesterday I'm walking down the Avenida of Seventy-Seven Years of Freedom and just imagine …
HEAD: (*Reassuringly.*) Yes, yes, we're imagining …
MARIA: Just imagine, a white Jaguar starts following me slowly, and the man driving is not so old at all …
HEAD: What a stroke of luck!
ALEXANDRO: Maria!
MARIA: Don't bother me! (*To the* Head.) That wasn't addressed to you. So you see, the man smiles at me and starts pressing buttons. Button number one is the twist, button number two the bossa-nova, button number three the hully-gully … And on the back seat of his car, just imagine, the biggest and most beautiful bottles. Can you imagine who it was?
HEAD: I know, do you?
MARIA: (*Solemnly.*) It was the Second Secretary to the Deputy Assistant to the Manager in Charge of the Department of Empty Containers at the Masculinus Company, that's who it was!
HEAD: And naturally, you ...
MARIA: (*In despair.*) Oh, I was still so stupid then. I believed that neurotic. (*Points to* Alexandro.)
HEAD: And now?
MARIA: Now I don't believe him. At this point in our lives, when ...
HEAD: That's right, for now, just stand in the corner by the proscenium.
GREGORO: (*Putting his hands in his pockets, nonchalantly saunters over to the* Head) I wish to make it clear that I am neither an avant-gardist nor a benighted traditionalist. I am an independent musician ...
HEAD: Sure, sure. We'll find a job for you too. Stand over there, next to her.
ALEXANDRO: (*Upset.*) What's going on here? Gregoro!
GREGORO: Try to understand, Alexandro. I was brought up in comfort, I'm used to elegant things. And what's more, I miss my girlfriend. (*He stands next to* Maria.)
HEAD: (*To* Miquelo.) We've got things worked out for you too. We

encourage abstract art.

MIQUELO: Personally I'm not an abstract artist, personally I'm ...

HEAD: That's O.K. You'll have time for creative soul-searching and breast-beating, for sleepless nights, everything as it ought to be. We'll even fix you up with salami and booze so you can get drunk as a skunk. Stand over there, with the others.

ALEXANDRO: Miquelo!

MIQUELO: Don't make a fuss, old boy. I can't go on starving here in the sand. No books to read, no cultural activities. And you've forgotten to include my girlfriend in the plot, old buddy. And as for the Freedom Tree, the results are zero. Sorry, old buddy!

HEAD: (*Briskly.*) By the numbers, sound off!

MARIA: One!

GREGORO: Two!

MIQUELO: One!

MARIA: Two!

GREGORO: One!

MIQUELO: Two!

MARIA: One!

GREGORO: Two!

MIQUELO: One!

MARIA: Two!

HEAD: Form two columns!

(*After some confusion the enlisted personnel form two columns.*)

HEAD: Forward march! Sing out!

(*The enlisted personnel go out singing "Masculinus, Masculinus! "* Feodoro, *too, hastily attempts to leave the stage.*)

ALEXANDRO: And just where do you think you're going, Feodoro?

FEODORO: I must get back to my duties. (*Lowering his voice.*) Better not have anything to do with them, Alex. Don't play Don Quixote. (*He goes out. Only* Alexandro *and the* Head *remain on the stage.*)

ALEXANDRO: Now maybe you'll explain to me what all this means?

HEAD: And what exactly would you like to find out?..

(*The* Head *does not show the slightest interest in* Alexandro, *and in fact starts to roll slowly toward the back of the stage.*)

ALEXANDRO: You've barged into my plot, you've kidnapped my heroes and my sweetheart, and to top it all . .

HEAD: It's an intrusion by life, my dear fellow, an intrusion at one and the same time intricate and beautiful, enchanting and merciless. It's ordinary capitalist reality. Man is a wolf to man. Crunch! Crunch!

ALEXANDRO: Why don't you go straight to hell?

HEAD: To hell? With the greatest of pleasure ... (*Rolls offstage*)

ALEXANDRO: (*Yelling after it*) And where am I supposed to go?

HEAD: (*From offstage*) That is your business, my dear fellow, that is your business.

ALEXANDRO: (*Drags himself across the stage alone, wringing his hands in despair.*) Oh, what a disaster! Where did that vile creature come from? And why are those loathsome features so familiar to me? (*Goes over to the palm tree and shakes it*) I've been left all alone. Send me just anything, oh Freedom Tree. (*Shakes the palm tree.*) Nothing – a huge cipher! Must I really go back there to that other world?

(*The light goes out. End of the Prologue.*)

SCENE TWO

The rear of the stage shows the huge windows of a capitalist office. Gigantic letters spell MASCULINUS. In front of the office stand three white Jaguar convertibles with their radiators facing forward; they are breathtaking in their luxurious beauty.

By the proscenium, a rundown slum tenement. Alexandro sits in front of it. He is writing, working on a novel, but it is going very poorly – hunger is gnawing at his entrails. Alexandro is dressed in rags and looks completely exhausted. A Sandwich Man appears at the proscenium. On his chest and back hang signboards bearing the inscription: "Juiciest Sausages in the World. NAPOLEON THE THIRD. Recommended to All Gentlemen-Guardsmen."

ALEXANDRO: (*To the* Sandwich Man) Hey, pal, why don't you give a free artist a bite of sausage?
SANDWICH MAN: Haven't tasted one myself for three years.

(*The* Second Sandwich Man *appears, "BISMARCK BUTTER – The World's Best Cure for Dystrophy."*)

ALEXANDRO: (*To the* Second Sandwich Man) A pat of butter for the future Shakespeare!
SECOND SANDWICH MAN: Haven't tasted any butter myself for five years. For us down in shanty town, the temporary shortage is permanent.

(*The* Third Sandwich Man *appears. "NERO – The World's Best Rolls. Bread – The Best Sputnik for Circuses."*)

ALEXANDRO: (*To the* Third Sandwich Man) Hey, friend, give a little bite to the future genius of our country.
THIRD SANDWICH MAN: You must be out of your mind! Haven't eaten any bread myself for eighteen years!
ALEXANDRO: (*To the* Sandwich Men) Then what do you guys eat?
SANDWICH MEN: We boil
the soles
of our shoes.

(*We see that all three* Sandwich Men *are barefoot.*)

ALEXANDRO: (*Bitterly*) We simply don't want to open our eyes to the evils of capitalist reality!

(*The* Fourth Sandwich Man *appears dressed in a shiny uniform and with solidly built boots on his feet. He himself looks fresh and healthy: "The Masculinus Company Needs No Advertising. Drink our Incomparable Masculinus Whisky."*)

FOURTH SANDWICH MAN: (*To the* First, Second *and* Third Sandwich Men.) Want to feed your faces, boys?
SANDWICH MEN: And how!
FOURTH SANDWICH MAN: And have a drink or two?
SANDWICH MEN: You bet!
FOURTH SANDWICH MAN: Throw away those stupid signboards of yours!

(*The* Sandwich Men *throw away their signboards with a clatter.*)

FOURTH SANDWICH MAN: By the numbers, sound off!
SANDWICH MEN: One, two, one, two ...
FOURTH SANDWICH MAN: Form two columns! Forward march!

(*The* Sandwich Men *form two columns and march off.*)

FOURTH SANDWICH MAN: (*With a free and easy gait, goes to* Alexandro.) Say, what's your problem, free artist?
ALEXANDRO: Beat it!
FOURTH SANDWICH MAN: Kootchy-koo! Oh, you're our darling little, independent, apolitical ...
ALEXANDRO: Leave me alone!
FOURTH SANDWICH MAN: (*Suddenly rummaging through* Alexandro*'s manuscripts*) What are we writing here, what are we working on? (*Reads.*) What a gift of language! What an exquisite style! What a powerful imagination! "He saw an enormous palm tree and heard singing..."
ALEXANDRO: (*Jumping up in a frenzy.*) I'll teach you, you scum!
FOURTH SANDWICH MAN: (*Jumps to one side.*) Just whose singing did he hear? A donkey's? A billy-goat's? Or some girlie's?
ALEXANDRO: I'm weak from hunger, but I'll teach you a lesson anyhow, you dirty scum! Where have I seen that villainous mug of yours before?

(*The three* Sandwich Men, *wearing new boots and marching briskly, pass across the proscenium. They are carrying "Masculinus" placards.*)

FIRST SANDWICH MAN: Whisky, not meat!
SECOND SANDWICH MAN: Whisky, not butter!
THIRD SANDWICH MAN: Whisky, not bread!

(*They go out.*)

FOURTH SANDWICHMAN: That's a mighty pretty sight! Fills your heart with joy, to see people in new boots already feeling a little bit high. Live and learn, son of a Shakespeare!

ALEXANDRO: (*Sits down, completely exhausted*) I'd rather boil the soles of my shoes than work for your cursed company.

(*Takes off his shoes, pulls out a knife and begin to cut off the soles.*)

FOURTH SANDWICH MAN: Stupid, very stupid. The best brains in the country are already working for us. Just look at the cars they're driving.

ALEXANDRO: (*Venomously.*) The best? Do you really think so?

FOURTH SANDWICH MAN: (*Even more venomously.*) Maybe you think the best brains are writing for that magazine of yours, *The Southern Teetotaler*? Are you really counting on that pitiful bunch of impotent liberals? You imagine that if those lamebrains publish your great works ...

ALEXANDRO: You've turned ninety percent of my fellow citizens into idiots, but you won't succeed with me!

FOURTH SANDWICH MAN: (*Yells to the rear of the stage.*) Gentlemen Stockholders Holding the Controlling Share, he's afraid we'll turn him into an idiot!

(*One of the windows on the facade of the office opens and in it we see three important gentlemen – the* Stockholders *Holding the Controlling Share. In actual fact, they are the three* Sandwich Men.)

ALEXANDRO: Ha, that's a pretty quick transformation!

FOURTH SANDWICH MAN: See how people get ahead in our system?

FIRST STOCKHOLDER: Never fear that we'll besot you.

SECOND STOCKHOLDER: We won't besot you, have no fear.

THIRD STOCKHOLDER: Just work for us, please.

FIRST STOCKHOLDER: You can keep all your skepticism and irony. We need critical minds.

SECOND STOCKHOLDER: Hold on to all your dreams and high ideals. They'll come in handy.

THIRD STOCKHOLDER: Just work for us.

FIRST STOCKHOLDER: You can even hate our company in the depths of your soul.

SECOND STOCKHOLDER: And never touch a drop of alcohol.

THIRD STOCKHOLDER: Just work for us.

(*Without saying a word, Alexandro keeps on cutting off the soles of his shoes.*)

FOURTH SANDWICH MAN: Why don't you say something? Such enticing propositions! And anyhow, stand up when the Gentlemen Stockholders talk to you!

(*Without saying a word,* Alexandro *keeps on cutting off the soles of his shoes.*)

FOURTH SANDWICH MAN: (*To the* Stockholders.) A clinical case of feeble-mindedness, Señores.
FIRST STOCKHOLDER: It seems we'll have to have recourse ...
SECOND STOCKHOLDER: To other means.
THIRD STOCKHOLDER: But just don't make them too drastic. Youth, Señores, youth ...

(*The window closes.*)

FOURTH SANDWICH MAN: So long, pussy cat! (*Goes out*)

(*Without saying a word,* Alexandro *keeps on cutting off the soles of his shoes.* Feodoro *appears.*)

ALEXANDRO: (*Rushes to* Feodoro.) Feddy, at last you've come! What happened?
FEODORO: I don't have any news to cheer you up, Alex.
ALEXANDRO: Did they really reject me again? What are they doing to me, the vipers?
FEODORO: Don't get mad at them; they rejected you, but with sincere regrets. (*Gives the manuscript back to* Alexandro.)
ALEXANDRO: With sincere regrets! The hypocrites! What is there about my stories that doesn't suit them?
FEODORO: At the *Southern Teetotaler* they think you're somewhat overinclined to the North, and at the *Northern Beer Drinker* they told me you lean too much to the South.
ALEXANDRO: (*In despair.*) In that case, take it to the *Equatorial Alcoholic!* What a hideous situation!
FEODORO: (*Cautiously.*) And do you really think that the *Equatorial Alcoholic* will be eager to publish you? Add a couple of drinking bouts, a word or two about Masculinus – it won't change the meaning, but everyone will understand what's what.
ALEXANDRO: Listen, Feodoro, you're open-hearted, you're high-minded, and what's more important – you're clear-headed. You feel the same way I do, you consider yourself my friend. So mark my words – never in my life will I cross the threshold of the *Equatorial Alcoholic!* (*He finally finishes cutting off the soles of his shoes, puts the saucepan on the burner, and throws the soles into it.*)
FEODORO: (*Horror-stricken.*) What are you doing?
ALEXANDRO: (*Proudly.*) I am boiling the soles of my shoes!
FEODORO: How could you ever sink so low! You look absolutely frightful! You'll destroy your talent and yourself along with it. One more week of this and you'll be finished. You ought to settle down and take a job. Look how nicely your friends Gregoro and Miquelo are getting along.

ALEXANDRO: I've heard they're working for Masculinus, is that so?
FEODORO: And what's wrong with that? A person can work wherever he feels like, the important thing is to stick to one's convictions. You know, Gregoro and Miquelo are even subscribing to the *Southern Teetotaler*. Of course, they don't broadcast the fact, they don't cast pearls before swine ...
ALEXANDRO: You can all go to hell along with your *Southern Teetotaler!*
FEODORO: (*Timidly crossing his legs.*) You're going downhill, don't roll all the way ...
ALEXANDRO: I'll cut your ears off and your snide liberal tongue too. I'll boil them up along with the soles of my shoes and be sated for two whole days.

(*Moves threateningly towards* Feodoro *with his knife.*)

FEODORO: Wait a minute, pal, let me ask you one last question. Where is Maria?
ALEXANDRO: (*Drops his hands.*) I have no idea. Paradise in a little thatched hut doesn't appeal to her. She's worried about losing her figure.
FEODORO: She's taken a job.
ALEXANDRO: Maria too ...?
FEODORO: Yes. She's working for the Advertising Department at the Masculinus Company, just like Gregoro and Miquelo.
ALEXANDRO: (*Bitterly.*) Her I can understand. There's a bit of the prostitute in every attractive woman. (*He lapses into silence; then, as if determined, raises his head up.*) Feodoro, I agree to take a job.
FEODORO: (*Joyfully.*) At last! I'm happy for you!
ALEXANDRO: But not for Masculinus. Help me at least to get started in your stinking Half-Strength Beer Trust.
FEODORO: (*Hesitatingly.*) Oh, yes ... hm ... hmm ... But, you see, the Trust is actually in a shaky situation and for the time being job-openings are ... Did you read the morning papers? They say Bismarck went bankrupt, Napoleon the Third has crashed. Nero has one foot in the grave. But don't think that I'm not willing to put in a good word for you. I'm willing to. But for now, try and understand ... You see, perhaps you should think about other possibilities. So long, Alex. (*Goes out.*)
ALEXANDRO: Too bad I didn't cut off the soles of his shoes. (*Sits down by the saucepan, stirs it, boils his soles.*)

(*The window opens. The same three* Stockholders *Holding the Controlling Share appear in it.*)

FIRST STOCKHOLDER: The following bulletin has just been received from the Internal Intelligence Agency. Yesterday in the waterfront district a five-year old hooligan wrote on one of our advertising posters: "Alcohol Destroys Your Health."

SECOND STOCKHOLDER: We should check on the work of the Advertising Department.

THIRD STOCKHOLDER: How are your youngsters doing there? Our golden pride?

(*The* Stockholders *press a button. Three windows open;* Gregoro *appears in the first,* Miquelo *in the second,* Maria *in the third.*)

GREGORO: To the Stockholders Holding the Controlling Share, on behalf of the Advertising Department

MIQUELO: Greetings!

MARIA: And a kiss!

FIRST STOCKHOLDER: Well?

SECOND STOCKHOLDER: Let's have your report.

THIRD STOCKHOLDER: How are you feeling, youngsters?

MIQUELO: Last night I climbed up the TV tower with a group of mountain climbers and drew the trademark of our product on the national flag in indelible paint ...

FIRST STOCKHOLDER: Bold and romantic. It's a pity you weren't shot on the spot. You'd have become our martyr and hero forever.

MIQUELO: I regret it deeply myself.

SECOND STOCKHOLDER: We must shove a bill through Parliament to have our trademark made part of the national flag.

MARIA: (*Picking up the telephone receiver.*) Parliament? I'm calling from the Masculinus Company. (*To the Stockholders.*) That got them hustling all right.

GREGORO: I bought the Philharmonic Orchestra lock, stock and barrel. I've composed an oratorio for it. In a week, on Memorial Day for the Victims of the Sixth World War, the orchestra will perform my oratorio in the National Cemetery. It opens with the following song:

Masculinus – to drink I'm always keen,
Masculinus – it's fit for King or Queen,
Masculinus – on hand in every bar,
Masculinus – smoother than honey by far.

THIRD STOCKHOLDER: Not bad! Splendid! A thoroughly captivating melody!

MARIA: (*Laughing, puts down the receiver*) They heard Gregoro's song in Parliament. Now the Speaker of the House is yelling at the top of his lungs.

FIRST STOCKHOLDER: (*Leaning out the window, chucks Maria under the chin.*) And what about you, my little girl? What have you accomplished?

MARIA: I've organized a society of Young Bacchantes at the University. And the outlying areas are following the lead of the students in the capital. I think that in a month's time there'll be a broad network of these societies throughout the country, and by spring we'll organize a Nationwide Bacchanalia.

FIRST STOCKHOLDER: (*In a low tone of voice.*) If you ask me, she's our most talented employee.

SECOND STOCKHOLDER: (*Venomously.*) You should know.

THIRD STOCKHOLDER: The most talented, naturally, the most enterprising, the most ... (*Chokes with delight.*)

FIRST STOCKHOLDER: Friends, the Council of the Stockholders takes note of the good work of the Advertising Department. But at the same time the Council also takes note of certain deficiencies in the coverage of the total population ... Give some thought to the possibility of organizational work among preschool children. There are disturbing signs from the cities. Yesterday in the waterfront district a five-year old hooligan wrote on one of our posters: "Alcohol Destroys Your Health." Give some thought to introducing our product into the kindergarten system.

MARIA, MIQUELO and GREGORO: We'll certainly give it some thought.

SECOND STOCKHOLDER: The meeting is adjourned.

THIRD STOCKHOLDER: Take it easy, youngsters.

(Maria, Miquelo *and* Gregoro *jump down from the window straight into the drivers seats of their white Jaguars. The* Stockholders *Holding the Controlling Share watch their departure in a fatherly fashion. The motors start up.* Maria, Miquelo *and* Gregoro *with shining faces drive off singing*):

> We're your soldiers, Masculinus!
> Masculinus, to battle lead us!
> Our rivals we'll obliterate,
> All barriers eliminate!
> Victorious thunder resound,
> Masculinus expound!

(*They drive on, shining and exchanging dazzling smiles. The* Stockholders *wave at them lovingly.*)

FIRST STOCKHOLDER: Splendid youth, all our hopes go with you.

SECOND STOCKHOLDER: Your hopes, I hope, are also our hopes.

THIRD STOCKHOLDER: Enterprising youth, militant youth, such wonderful youth! (*Chokes with delight.*)

(*During all this, at the proscenium* Alexandro *has dozed off beside his saucepan. He dreams the doomed dream of an outcast. In the office the teletype machine has started working.*)

SECOND STOCKHOLDER: (*Reads the teletype.*) More alarming news again. The Internal Intelligence Agency reports the following: Today after receiving their pay, 57.5 percent of the workers at the Summer Parasol Factory passed straight by our bars on their way to the Savings Bank.

THIRD STOCKHOLDER: That's simply terrible! I'm very frightened of the proletariat! (*Hiccups from excitement.*)

SECOND STOCKHOLDER: And there's more! 44.6 percent of the employees at the Agricultural Department after receiving their pay content themselves with only half-strength beer.

THIRD STOCKHOLDER: That's simply terrible! I start trembling at the very thought of the intelligentsia and the peasant class! (*Hiccups more violently.*)

SECOND STOCKHOLDER: (*Gloomily.*) The Foreign Intelligence Agency furnishes the following information: In New York on Broadway a spontaneous demonstration took place under the banner: "Masculinus go home!"

THIRD STOCKHOLDER: That's simply terrible! I get in a state of panic whenever I hear of people's wars of liberation!

FIRST STOCKHOLDER: (*Harshly.*) Stop that hiccuping!

THIRD STOCKHOLDER: (*Bursts out sobbing.*) You don't like me! You don't feel sorry for me! You despise me!

FIRST STOCKHOLDER: (*In a cold voice.*) Stop hiccuping and sobbing at the same time! (*The* Third Stockholder *stops.*) We've got to take immediate countermeasures. In the first place, it's time to finish off that wretched Half-Strength Beer Trust. In the second place, we must exert pressure on the government so they'll lodge a protest with that pitiful United States ... After all, the U.S. is just a paper tiger. With our cavalry regiments ... No more of that now. In the third place, friends, no matter what you say, we've got to strengthen our Advertising Department. Of course, those youngsters are doing their job well, but what we need is a genius, a real brain, a superman, an inventor, a Newton, an Einstein, a Spinoza. That's what. Now, get down to business.

(*The window closes. On stage rushing cars, at the proscenium* Alexandro, *dozing.*)

GREGORO: What are we going to do? We've got to do something.

MIQUELO: Well, anything except drink that stinking Masculinus! What do you say to a stein of half-strength beer?

MARIA: (*Mischievously.*) Boys, I've got some Russian vodka.

GREGORO: Quiet! Have you gone crazy? Not a word about Russia.

MIQUELO: We'll go to your house, but we've got to be quiet.

MARIA: We'll have a quiet little shot.

(*The drive continues.* Alexandro *wakes up, rushes over to the saucepan which is boiling over, takes it off the flame, and tries the broth.*)

ALEXANDRO: What a hearty broth! What's the secret? Ah, you see the whole secret lies in the fact that here, stuck to the sole of my shoe, there's a piece of sausage skin, and a lemon peel, and even a bay leaf. Ha, ha, ha! Hey, all you starving of the world! You've got soup right under your feet! (*Eats with great appetite.*) It needs more salt. (*He takes off both his socks and dips them in the saucepan, tastes the soup and lets out a desperate scream.*) What an idiot, I've oversalted it! Now it's inedible. What'll I do? I'll really die from hunger now ... (*For a while he remains perplexed, crushed by sorrow, then screams furiously.*) Oh, no, I'll never kiss Masculinus's ass! Cursed ass, all sugary, and soft and sweet like a layer-cake! That ass hangs over me and tempts me – kiss me, kiss me, you'll become rich and famous! Fat chance! I'll bite you, cursed ass, stinking of all the goodies in the world! (*Bites an imaginary ass.*) I'd rather go off to the jungle and turn savage! I'll eat lizards and other crawling reptiles! I'd rather become a gangster and be cut down by hired assassins' bullets! I'd rather be a pimp for waterfront whores!

(*Three* Policemen *appear at the proscenium. In actual fact, they are the same as the* Sandwich Men *and the* Stockholders.)

FIRST POLICEMAN: Here is a directive from the municipal administration. (*Reads*): At a recent session of the Council the following determination has been reached: Slum-dwellings and shanty towns are disgraceful blemishes on the beautiful face of our perennially flowering capital. These eyesores impede the advertising campaigns of our leading companies. It has therefore been resolved: To single out slums and wipe them off the face of the earth. Implementation of the directive is to be carried out by a special police unit.

SECOND POLICEMAN: As a leading expert on the subject I have reached the following determination: This slum dwelling is a typical dilapidated tenement. Condemned to be razed to the ground.

THIRD POLICEMAN: Too bad, such a picturesque slum, but what can you do about it!

FIRST POLICEMAN: Get to work, boys!

(*The* policemen *set to work destroying the slum.*)

ALEXANDRO: What are you doing? This is where I live! Hands off! My home is my castle! (*The slum is destroyed.*)

ALEXANDRO: Then you have to provide me with a one-room apartment with all the modern conveniences.

FIRST POLICEMAN: Let's see your papers!

(Alexandro *produces his passport. The* First Policeman *examines it.*)

SECOND POLICEMAN: (*Looking over the* First Policeman's *shoulder.*) Are all the stamps properly affixed? Is the left footprint there?
THIRD POLICEMAN: (*Looking over the* Second Policeman's *shoulder.*) The photograph doesn't match. The photo shows a chubby little fellow with freckles and a big, wide smile, but the bearer of this passport is nothing but a ragged skeleton.
FIRST POLICEMAN: (*To* Alexandro.) Just what do you do for a living?
ALEXANDRO: I'm a writer.
SECOND POLICEMAN: Where do you work?
ALEXANDRO: Nowhere. I write fiction.
THIRD POLICEMAN: (*In mock horror.*) Well, well, well, an honest-to-god parasite in our midst?
ALEXANDRO: I'm not a parasite. I write fiction.

(*The* Policemen *start to roar with laughter. They simply can't control themselves.* Alexandro *is completely at a loss.*)

ALEXANDRO: I repeat – I'm a writer.
FIRST POLICEMAN: Oh, I'm just dying from laughter – a writer.
SECOND POLICEMAN: He writes fiction – would you believe it?
THIRD POLICEMAN: What a disgrace! Parasites in our perenially flowering capital!
ALEXANDRO: (*Hysterically.*) I'm not a parasite! I write fiction!
FIRST POLICEMAN: (*Getting serious.*) Do you have a certified statement declaring your source of income? How much did you earn last year from your – what did you call it ...?
SECOND POLICEMAN: Fiction, ooh-ooh-ha-ha ...
THIRD POLICEMAN: Fiction – friction – jurisdiction – crucifixion. You'd be better off writing poetry, young man.
ALEXANDRO: (*Gloomily.*) I haven't earned any money from my writing. Not a single penny. But I'm not a parasite. I write fiction.
FIRST POLICEMAN: Since you write …
SECOND POLICEMAN: Fiction.
THIRD POLICEMAN: That's right. Since you write that ... that stuff you were talking about, it means you ought to understand that ... what do you call it …
THIRD POLICEMAN: Logic.
FIRST POLICEMAN: Exactly. Since you write that other stuff, it means you ought to understand this stuff, you know. If you haven't earned anything from that stuff of yours, and you don't work anywhere, it means you're living off unearned income. And that means you're a parasite.
ALEXANDRO: I don't have any unearned income.
THIRD POLICEMAN: Just what are you eating, buddy?

ALEXANDRO: I'm cooking the soles of my own shoes.
SECOND POLICEMAN: But where did you get money for the shoes?
ALEXANDRO: (*Taken aback.*) You know, I ... there was a time when I didn't write fiction. Before, when I didn't write fiction ...
FIRST POLICEMAN: Look here, boy, don't think we're so easy to fool. We know all about you. You always wrote that stuff.
SECOND POLICEMAN: Don't you dare deny it – you always wrote fiction.
THIRD POLICEMAN: You can't hide anything from us, kid. Nowadays we've got very sophisticated ways of gathering information. Since you were a little child, you've always been fooling around with that fiction, and you've wasted a lot of paper. Better admit it.
ALEXANDRO: I'm not a parasite.
FIRST POLICEMAN: Call the witness.

(*Enters the witness, an elderly* Man of Independent Means.)

THIRD POLICEMAN: Here is a sterling witness. A senior citizen, a man of independent means, a model taxpayer, a man who never says no to a drink.
SECOND POLICEMAN: (*To the witness.*) Do you know this man?
MAN OF INDEPENDENT MEANS: Of course, I don't know the person in question, I never set eyes on him, I never read one word of his fiction – I don't have anything in common with him, officers. I can only say this: It is not fit and decent for parasites to dirty the spotlessly clean sidewalks of our perennially flowering capital with their presence! Down with idlers and spongers, throw them out of our perennially flowering capital!
FIRST POLICEMAN: (*To* Alexandro.) Do you hear the voice of the people speaking?
ALEXANDRO: I'm not a parasite!
THIRD POLICEMAN: (*In astonishment.*) Then just who are you?
ALEXANDRO: I'm a fiction writer!
POLICEMEN and MAN OF INDEPENDENT MEANS: Ooh-ha-ha! Ooh-ha-ha!

(*At the rear of the stage* Feodoro *peddles by on his bicycle somberly. The briefcase of a typical functionary is attached to the bicycle frame.*)

ALEXANDRO: (*Noticing* Feodoro.) Here's my witness! Now he'll tell you who I am! Feodoro! Feddy! Come here!

(*He rushes towards* Feodoro, *but the* Policemen *hold him back.* Feodoro *peddles off without even hearing* Alexandro's *screams.*)

FIRST POLICEMAN: Look here, you son-of-a-bitch, we're giving you twenty-four minutes to pack your belongings. Soon you'll have lizards for your next door neighbors on the desert in Cuco-Fuego. And if you try to escape, we'll send you to the galleys. Get ready to travel, fictioneer clipped-to-the ear! (*Goes out.*)

SECOND and THIRD POLICEMEN: Fiction writer! Oooh-ha-ha! Oooh-ha-ha! (*They go out.*)

ALEXANDRO: (*Grabs his manuscripts and dashes around the stage like a madman.*) The whole world's taken arms against me! I'm finished! I won't be able to stand this humiliation! Better throw myself under the wheels of a moving car! Farewell, Maria! Farewell, my friends! My time has come!

(*Rushes to meet the headlights of the three Jaguars which are bearing straight down on him.*)

MARIA: Some filthy ragamuffin is running straight at us!

GREGORO: Slam on the brakes!

MIQUELO: Too late!

(Alexandro *throws himself directly under the wheels. The brakes squeal.* Maria *screams.* Gregoro *and* Miquelo *jump out of their cars and pull* Alexandro's *body from under the wheels.*)

MARIA: Alexandro! (*She faints momentarily but immediately comes to.*) You look just terrible! My God, he hasn't shaved for days!

MIQUELO: Alex, my friend!

GREGORO: Are you all right, Alexandro? Are you alive?

ALEXANDRO: Am I really alive? Look, my arms and legs are all in one piece, so I must be OK? Boys, is it you! Maria, is it you? Maria! My baby! Look at me, boys – I'm alive! Life is beautiful! To hell with it all, I want to live, live, live, drive a car like yours, sleep with Maria! I want to eat! I want to drink! I want to get my fill of that rotten Masculinus and dance the twist with Maria! Hurrah! I'm alive!

MARIA: At last you've finally come to your senses! Climb into the car next to me!

(Alexandro *climbs into the car next to her. They kiss.*)

GREGORO and MIQUELO: Hurrah! Alexandro has joined us! Full speed ahead!

(*The headlights have been turned on. The Jaguars race on ahead.* Feodoro *runs onto the stage.*)

FEODORO: (*Yells.*) Alexandro, is that you? I've got news that'll upset you – our trust has gone bankrupt. I'm out of work!

ALEXANDRO: To hell with it, the devil take your trust! I'm starting a new life! All that literary nonsense can go straight to the devil. (*Flings all his manuscripts away.*)

GREGORO, MIQUELO and MARIA: (*Sing*)

We're your soldiers, Masculinus!
Masculinus, to battle lead us!
Our rivals we'll obliterate,
All barriers eliminate!
Victorious thunder resound,
Masculinus expound!

(Alexandro *joins in the singing.* Feodoro *sadly picks up the manuscripts.*)

Curtain

SCENE THREE

On stage, the office of the Advertising Department at the Masculinus Company. TV sets, teletype machines, wall-shelves. A wide window through which can be seen a typical capitalist landscape with skyscrapers.

Above the window, in large letters, the master slogan:

MAN IS A WOLF, HYENA, LEOPARD TO MAN!

Lower, down, in a various places, lesser slogans:

DIVIDE AND GOVERN!

FIRST THE WHIP, THEN THE HONEY CAKE!

BY HOOK OR BY CROOK!

WHISKY, NOT

BUTTER!

MEAT!

BREAD!

FISH!

BEER!

WHISKY, NOT GUNS!

In the corner, there hangs a chart on which is written:

YESTERDAY TODAY TOMORROW DAY-AFTER TOMORROW

Alexandro *and* Maria *dance the twist in the middle of the stage.* Alexandro *is dressed in a chic white outfit. General air of foppishness and prosperity.* Gregoro *is sitting in a chair with his legs crossed.* Miquelo *sprawls on the window sill.*

MIQUELO: (*Recounting.*) Yesterday I was reading this book – a real dazzler! Full of one allusion after the other. Here's how it goes. There's this girl, some sort of nymphette, who goes out into the forest, wearing a red hood. Did you get the allusion?

GREGORO: Oh-ho-ho.

MARIA: (*To* Alexandro.) One of those old fogeys, one of the Principal Stockholders, has taken fancy to me.

ALEXANDRO: Ha-ha, well, if I get my hands on him, I'll kill him.

MIQUELO: And then this sort of Wolf comes out and meets the girl, it's an obvious allegory, in other words, a sex-champion comes out to meet her with his pink jaws wide open ...

GREGORO: Then what happened?

MARIA: But why kill him, honey! Just think - he pats me on the bottom once a day - I don't mind, and he enjoys it a lot. Anyhow, he isn't capable of anything more.

ALEXANDRO: All right, I won't kill him. Have it your way,

MIQUELO: At one point he almost devoured the poor girl. Understand, he nearly gobbled her up.

GREGORO: So now they call it gobbling up?

MARIA: What? I'll gobble him up! One snap – that's all.

(*They finish dancing and sprawl in chairs.*)

GREGORO: (*Yawning.*) Well, what do you say, friends, shall we do a little work for our enchanting company and may they all drop dead?

MIQUELO: (*Stretching.*) Yesterday in East Africa a detachment of our goons intercepted a van full of yogurt and smashed all the bottles. They do their work a bit roughly.

MARIA: The Department of Overseas Operations is nothing but the worst goons and bandits.

ALEXANDRO: In any big operation you can't get along without bandits.

GREGORO: Be quiet, boys, suppose the Stockholders overhear us.

ALEXANDRO: Let them. They don't give a damn about your opinions, as long as we do our work well. After all, they're jackasses.

MIQUELO: They're pigs.

GREGORO: They've got appetites like pigs.

MARIA: And lustful desires like billy-goats.

ALEXANDRO: At least they pay us well.

(*A section of the stage opens; within the* Stockholders *can be seen giggling.*)

THIRD STOCKHOLDER: Oh, you madcaps!

SECOND STOCKHOLDER: Is that the way you treat us?

FIRST STOCKHOLDER: And now off you go to work. Mischievous children! Any new ideas, Señor Alexandro?

ALEXANDRO: I've just thought up something.

FIRST STOCKHOLDER: Boy, oh, boy, oh, boy! (*The* Third Stockholder *gasps for breath from overexcitement.*)

ALEXANDRO: With respect to the problem of serving the sick and aged. It is clear that so far we have not successfully resolved this question. A sick person desirous of ordering whisky sent to his home is obliged to dial zero, zero, zero, zero, zero, zero, zero, zero. Just imagine the great distance that his sick, trembling finger must travel from zero to the stop-bar! And eight times at that! I propose changing our number to eight ones. In this manner we shall immediately increase the number of orders many times over, and the sick people will benefit greatly. And it would be even better if the order number were simply one, only one one, instead of eight ones! A flip of the finger and whisky flows to your heart's content.

FIRST STOCKHOLDER: One is the number reserved for the Emergency Ambulance Service. That's the hitch!

ALEXANDRO: Emergency Ambulance Service can be eliminated. What uninspired altruism. Some idiotic Emergency Ambulance Service handed down to us from the times of uninspired altruism! We must think about the health of the whole nation, not just about some of its individual members. To hell with Emergency Ambulance Service!

SECOND STOCKHOLDER: Hmm ... yes. Conflict with the government is possible.

ALEXANDRO: (*In an offended tone of voice.*) Well, you know the best. My business is to propose ...

THIRD STOCKHOLDER: We appreciate your proposal very much, but ... (*In a whisper.*) We've got to give him some encouragement.

MARIA: (*Springing into action.*) So the proposal has been accepted? (*Picks up the telephone receiver.*)

FIRST STOCKHOLDER: Make a call.

MARIA: (*Speaking into the receiver.*) Department of Decision - Implementation? Hi there, boys! (*Laughs.*) What business, boys? (*Laughs.*) Is that you, Ambrosio? Don't be fresh. (*Laughs.*) What business is that of yours? (*Laughs.*) Shake the dirt out of your ears! (*Laughs.*) You won't get any. (*Laughs.*) Hooligan! (*Laughs.*) I forgot! The proposal has been accepted: The government is destined for the dust-bin of history. Quite literally. Spring into action! (*Laughs.*) Ambrosio, you're a hooligan and your whole Department's nothing but a bunch of fresh guys. (*Hangs up the telephone receiver.*) All taken care of!

FIRST STOCKHOLDER: (*To* Gregoro.) Turn on the television, my good man. We'll see how the situation is developing.

THIRD STOCKHOLDER: The government was nice, friendly, anxious to please ...

(Gregoro *turns on the television lackadaisically. On the screen a rampaging mob and the smoke of gunfire can be seen.*)

ANNOUNCER: (*Yelling excitedly.*) At this moment a crowd of drunken hooligans is storming the presidential palace. The government is calling in tanks from the National Guard to drive away the raging hordes.

(Gregoro *turns off the television.*)

FIRST STOCKHOLDER: (*To* Alexandro.) Let's continue the meeting. What measures do you propose with respect to preschool children?
SECOND STOCKHOLDER: With respect to unruly preschool children?
ALEXANDRO: In this instance we should adopt a responsive and enlightened educational policy. We should provide for change. At the very least every child should grow up to become a confirmed adult-user of Masculinus whisky.

(Gregoro *turns on the television.*)

ANNOUNCER: The tanks won't start. The Guardsmen are drunk. Detachments of hot-blooded inhabitants of our perennially flowering capital are continuing the siege of the governmental palace.
GREGORO: (*Turns off the television.*) This day will go down in history. I feel a symphony about to be born within me.
FIRST STOCKHOLDER: (*To* Miquelo.) It would be a good idea to create a huge battle canvas commemorating this day.
MIQUELO: I'm already planning the composition.
SECOND STOCKHOLDER: Go on. Señor Alexandro.
ALEXANDRO: Masculinus principles, Masculinus philosophy, Masculinus aesthetics should enter into the consciousness of each and every child starting with those in diapers. In all our kindergartens. Gentlemen Stockholders, your picture should be prominently displayed, with little children on your laps.
THIRD STOCKHOLDER: With little children on our laps! How marvelous! The cute, little rosy-cheeked darlings!! Our only hope and joy! (*Chokes with emotion.*)
ALEXANDRO: Small doses of whisky in their milk, in their cocoa, and in their cream of wheat, not only will do no harm to the development of youthful organisms, but on the contrary will contribute to their speedy growth and foster in children the daily need for Masculinus. The next question is broadcasting for children. Turn on the television, Gregoro.

(Gregoro *turns on the television.*)

ANNOUNCER: (*Joyfully.*) And the rotten and corrupt government has been thrown on the dustbin of history. The First Decree of the Provisional

Revolutionary Committee has abolished the Institute of Emergency Ambulance Service. The gang of barren altruists who had become entrenched in the Institute has been unmasked. And now a program for our small friends. We begin with the song: "Tell me, little birdie ..." (*Sings.*)

> Tell me, little birdie,
> What do you buy
> To wet your whistle
> When it is dry?
>
> Finchy-winchy?
> Why so frisky?
> Been to "Masculinus"
> To drink whisky.
> Had one shot, and then two more,
> And now my head is on the floor.

MARIA: They already got the message. Oh, look - behind the Announcer's back, it's Ambrosio with a revolver in his hand! Oh, that Ambrosio's a riot!

(Gregoro *turns off the television.*)

ALEXANDRO: They got the message, but not entirely. The end of that song, which isn't half bad, should go like this:

> Drank some whisky, felt like new,
> Punched the teacher black and blue.

Now turn it on, Gregoro.

(Gregoro *turns on the television.*)

ANNOUNCER: (*Scared to death.*) Now, children, memorize the refrain:

> Finchy-winchy, why so frisky!
> Been to "Masculinus" to drink whisky.
> Drank some whisky, felt like new,
> Punched the teacher, black and blue.

(Gregoro *turns off the television.*)

SECOND STOCKHOLDER: Quite a productive day! We're very pleased with you, Señor Alexandro.

THIRD STOCKHOLDER: A marvelous day! It warms one's heart! You are a splendid worker, Alex, if I may call you by your first name.

ALEXANDRO: All that's just for the time being, temporary measures.

FIRST STOCKHOLDER: Do you have something else in mind?

ALEXANDRO: The dissemination of our product and of our principles must be all-embracing and global in scope. The entire population must have absolutely deep and abiding faith in Masculinus. At all the difficult moments of life people should turn to Masculinus for consolation, and on joyous occasions all the more so, and in order for this to happen ...
STOCKHOLDERS: What do we need?
ALEXANDRO: In order for this to happen we need an idol. We must create a symbolic citizen devoted to Masculinus, who will be a favorite with all classes of society.
FIRST STOCKHOLDER: How much time do you need?
ALEXANDRO: About fifteen minutes.
FIRST STOCKHOLDER: Go to it.

(*The wall closes up.* Alexandro *holds his head in his hands and sinks down in his chair.* Maria *runs over to him.*)

MARIA: What's the matter with you, darling? You worked so wonderfully today ...
ALEXANDRO: Oh, I've got an awful headache!
MARIA: Take care of your head. Your head is a national treasure. (*She strokes his head.*)
ALEXANDRO: Guys, I keep having a strange dream - there's this tiny, little island in the middle of the ocean, and on it grows a single palm tree all by itself, but gigantic and generous, and all four of us are there, under that palm tree, joyful and free ...
MARIA: What sort of a strange dream is that?
ALEXANDRO: Oh, I've got an awful headache!
MIQUELO: How should we interpret that story? A tiny, little island and a single palm tree all by itself? What's the hidden meaning?
GREGORO: You really don't get it? (*Whispers something into* Miquelo's *ear.*)
MIQUELO: (*Roars with laughter.*) Aha! So that's it! You sure dressed that up cleverly!
ALEXANDRO: Oh, my head is splitting.
MARIA: What's the matter with you today, my darling? (*Kisses him.*)
ALEXANDRO: (*Pushing her aside; weakly.*) His name is Pork Sausage.
ALL: Whose name?
ALEXANDRO: (*Jumping up.*) Pork Sausage! He's our idol! Pork Sausage! A sweet kid! In himself he typifies all the swinishness of the average citizen, all the vulgarity, all the philistinism, all the current catch words and even the filthy language; he'll be our jester - impudent enough and just obliging enough, one of the boys, someone you can talk to and tell your troubles to. In all the magazines there'll be interviews with Pork; Pork's thoughts and sayings will appear in print everywhere; in all the movie theaters animated cartoons about Pork will be serialized - he'll get into every nook

and cranny, he'll become a part of our intimate, personal life. Old buddy Pork with his inseparable bottle of Masculinus. He'll remake all of life and transform the country into a cozy little madhouse. Pork Sausage!

MARIA: Brilliant! Simply brilliant! And what will Pork's relationship with women be?

ALEXANDRO: He'll be the idol of all the women; he'll give advice to housewives; he'll seduce the beauties and console the ugly ducklings. Under his influence women will make drunkards out of their husbands and lovers - they'll start guzzling whisky themselves. Miquelo, get to work on Pork's portrait; depict his charming, mocking snout, his little hook-like hands, his funny hat, his shabby-flabby suit. Don't forget - Pork is an ordinary citizen; there are millions like him. Gregoro, write a song, "Sing along with Pork."

GREGORO and MIQUELO: We're getting going.

ALEXANDRO: Maria, get a hold of the TV, the radio, the Municipal Office, the publishing houses, the newspapers and magazines.

MARIA: In a flash. Oh, we'll get things humming. (*Dashes to the telephone.*)

(*In the corner* Gregoro *works on the song.* Miquelo *with broad strokes draws on the wall a preposterous little man in a funny hat.*)

ALEXANDRO: (*Looking on.*) That's it, Miq. Wonderful.

MIQUELO: Should he have a little moustache, Alex?

ALEXANDRO: Unquestionably. And glasses. And a bottle in his back pocket.

MARIA: (*Shouts into the receiver.*) His name is Pork Sausage, you blockheads! I'll spell it for you: P as in Pig, O as in Oil, R as in Rape, K as in Kick ...

GREGORO: Should the song be just a tiny bit sentimental?

ALEXANDRO: Just the tiniest little bit.

MARIA: (*Into the receiver.*) Just one more piece of information. The ban on obscene expressions has been lifted. (*Laughs.*) Alex, they want to know if that includes even the word "dink"?

ALEXANDRO: Even "dinked-off"!

MARIA: Even "dinked-off"!

ALEXANDRO: Even "up the dinking dinker"!

MARIA: (*Into the receiver.*) Even "up the dinking dinker"! (*Laughs.*) Alex, those old hypocrites are trembling in their boots!

MIQUELO: Look, it's done.

ALEXANDRO: (*Examines the portrait carefully.*) You got it perfectly, Miq. I recognized him immediately. I've seen that face somewhere before. (*Shouts.*) Attention everyone, I'm about to give Pork's first speech. Pork Sausage analyzes the takeover of the government. Maria, turn on the television.

(Maria *turns on the television. The mocking cartoon snout of* Pork Sausage *appears on the screen.*)

PORK SAUSAGE: (*Tips his hat slightly, smiles.*) Greetings, bottle-buddies, boon-companions, and all you mamselles! It's me, Pork Sausage, persona grata, your ordinary citizen. Hey, Bobo, Lola, Chiquito, recognize me? Whew, did my throat ever get dry, dink me in the dinker if it didn't! (*Guffaws, nips the bottle.*) This is the way to make things get better and better. Oh, that's good stuff, that Masculinus, dink it all, smooth and tasty, you bet your dinking dinked-off dinkers it is! Open your bottles and listen to what I've got to say, old Pork isn't such a stupid fool. (*Takes a nip.*) Here's what I want to tell you about our former government. Now it goes without saying that those guys were bright and well educated. They just weren't so strong at drinking; after a snort or two they got sozzled. (*Guffaws, takes another nip.*) Every fruit has its season, but those guys got a little rotten, they must have smelled it themselves. So it turns out you're walking down the street past the government palace and it hits you in the nose so strong that you suddenly have to run to the nearest Masculinus bar, and tell the bartender, "Give me a triple." It was a stinking government, you can say that again, dink your dinking dinked-up dinker. Well, Bobo, Lola, Chiquito, how about it, pals? Got a little pie-eyed already? Oh, you're my bosom buddies. Do you respect me? I respect you. (*Drinks.*)

GREGORO: The song's ready.

ALEXANDRO: Let's see, Gregoro.

PORK SAUSAGE: And now pals, I'll sing you a little song. Learn it by heart. (*Sings.*)

Living like moles
In your small apartment holes.
Pop a cork,
Drink with Pork,
Eat with Pork
Pop a cork,

Living like moles
In your small apartment holes.
Old Pork will always lend you a hand -
The man on whom the world depends -
All problems he can understand,
He'll help with love and making friends.
Our happiness lies in the fight,
Stock up on supplies of whisky.
Old Pork will help when nothing's right.
With Pork the outcome's never risky.

Living like moles
In your small apartment holes,
Pop a cork,
Drink with Pork,
Sleep with Pork,
Eat with Pork
Pop a cork,
Living like moles
In your small apartment holes.

GREGORO: What do you think of the song?

ALEXANDRO: Just terrific. You're the greatest, Gregoro.

PORK SAUSAGE: Here's to you, Bobo, Lola, Chiquito! (*Drinks.*) So long for now. If that wasn't enough for you, just switch to channel two.

MARIA: (*Turns off the television.*) What a splendid monster! Congratulations, darling!

MIQUELO: (*Points out the window.*) Look at my work of art.

(*Through the window the audience can now see that on the roofs of all the skyscrapers there have appeared illuminated pictures of* Pork Sausage, *who makes faces and drinks down one shot glass after another.*)

ALEXANDRO: Just fabulous. Mary, how did the press respond?

MARIA: Why even ask? How could they respond, except the way we want?

ALEXANDRO: So all the evening papers will tell the entire nation about Pork. Sausage will analyze the most important issues of the day. There'll be round-table discussions between Sausage and workers, farmers, intellectuals, and individuals of independent means. Various articles about Pork Sausage will appear in all newspapers tomorrow. Neon ads have been put up, thanks to the efforts of our friend Miquelo. One hundred million copies of the Pork Sausage hit record will be released. Mary, get the telepathic transmitter ready. I'm going to broadcast Pork's speeches to all the Information Centers. Gregoro, Miquelo, you're free for the day, you can go home. Leave a few swigs of Russian vodka for Maria and me, we'll be getting back rather late.

GREGORO: Have you gone out of your mind? Talking out loud about Russia?

ALEXANDRO: I don't give a damn! We're doing such a great job for their rotten company we should feel free to say anything we want. Without us, their company would fall to pieces in a day or two. Mary, turn the transmitter on.

(Maria *turns the telepathic transmitter on.* Alexandro *settles down in front of it.* Gregoro *and* Miquelo *jump out through the window. Down below the engines of their cars have started humming.* Miquelo *and* Gregoro *sing:*)

We're your soldiers, Masculinus,
Masculinus, to battle lead us!

MARIA: (*Dances.*) Oh, I'm in such a good mood! How are those clever little ideas of yours, pussy cat? Flying around in your head like little birdies? You're my golden boy. I wonder how much money they'll pay you for Pork? Let's buy Jamaica, OK? Or the Bahamas? We'll run everything there just the way we want. We'll reorganize the whole place. We'll be awfully rich, darling.

(*Enter* Feodoro *with a newspaper in his hands. He looks around timidly.*)

MARIA: Oh, it's you Feodoro! What's new? Starving as usual?
FEODORO: Hi, Maria. No, I'm not starving anymore. I'm set up ... at Masculinus.
MARIA: Oh, so you sold out too?
FEODORO: I've got a family, Maria, and kids ... And besides I'm working for the Computer Department as an ordinary accountant ... I've got no connection with this snake pit ... Oh, Maria, I didn't mean that!
MARIA: Oh, that's right isn't it, you feel good once you've sold out. Until you actually do it, you feel kind of lousy, kind of uneasy, you're not quite yourself, but as soon as you sell out, right away you feel good. Right, Feddy?
FEODORO: I wanted to talk to Alexandro.
MARIA: He's busy. He's racking his brain for brilliant ideas.
ALEXANDRO: (*Getting up.*) That does it. All the newspapers have the articles now, and some of them have already come out.
FEODORO: Hi, Alex. That's just it. I'm here about the papers. Just picture this scene. I go down into the subway and what do I see? Everybody, absolutely everybody, is reading the Evening Rocker, they're all pleased as can be, chuckling, smiling, throwing their arms around one another, and swigging whisky straight from the bottle. Suddenly they've all become happy. I buy myself a newspaper and what do I find there - the outpourings of some idiotic Pork Sausage.
MARIA: Oho! Watch out! Idiotic! I suppose you're some great critical intelligence! Wretched little bookkeeper!
ALEXANDRO: They're quite the eager beavers over there at the "Evening Rocker"! Sharp boys.
FEODORO: (*Dumbfounded.*) Is that really your handiwork?
MARIA: (*Proudly.*) It was my Alex who thought up Pork Sausage.
FEODORO: No, I don't believe it! Was it really you? Just think what they're writing in that newspaper of theirs. (*Reads.*) "Your friend Pork Sausage explains the meaning of life." That's the headline. Now here's the story. "One fine day, old Pork dropped in on his neighbor, a philosopher, a kind

of uninspired altruist. 'What's the meaning of life, my friend?' Pork asked. 'I don't know," stammered the philosopher, that poor lost sheep. 'But I do,' said good, old Pork and pulled a bottle of Masculinus out of his back pocket. 'The meaning of life lies in the truth, my dear philosopher, and in vino veritas.' That was when the philosopher chucked his hopeless profession for good and all, and now he's working as a dishwasher in one of the Masculinus bars. He's well fed, drunk all the time, living in clover, and always keeps whistling some jaunty, optimistic tune. That's how our kind-hearted Pork helped that poor lost sheep." And so on and so forth ... ten stories about the meaning of life and all of them lead to the same ...

ALEXANDRO: You don't have to read any further. All of that is my doing.

FEODORO: (*Indignantly.*) I can't keep quiet! (*Whispers.*) Alexandro, just consider what a sordid business you're sacrificing your talent to. Why, in a few days that Pork of yours can turn the whole country into imbeciles.

ALEXANDRO: That's exactly our intention.

FEODORO: I'm ashamed for you. You've become completely demoralized.

ALEXANDRO: Wasn't it you who tried to convince me to work for Masculinus?

FEODORO: Yes, but I thought that you'd keep your ideals, that you wouldn't give up your writing ...

ALEXANDRO: You can go straight to the devil, all of you fine, noble souls! I've figured out the meaning of life too! I don't believe you! What use are you fighters for ideals! It's about the likes of you that one of the Russian poets wrote: "Lunch and supper, supper and lunch. That's good enough for the whole bunch."

FEODORO: He's gone completely crazy! Talking out loud about Russia? Want to get sent to prison?

ALEXANDRO: (*Bursts out laughing.*) You see for yourself what a coward you are!

MARIA: (*Attacking* Feodoro.) So you don't like our good, old boy, Pork Sausage?

FEODORO: (*Proudly.*) No!

MARIA: Do I hear you correctly? Say that again a little louder! You don't like the idol of the nation?

FEODORO: (*Growing frightened.*) No, why would I dislike him? He's not without his charm, that Pork of yours, but ...

MARIA: (*Threateningly.*) What does that "but" mean?

FEODORO: (*Speaking quite distinctly.*) I do like the idol of the nation, Pork Sausage. (*Hurriedly goes out.*)

MARIA: (*With her arms akimbo.*) Ha-ha-ha! He came around just in a nick of time. (*She turns around.* Alexandro *is lying in his chair as though he were sick.*) What's the matter with you, darling?

ALEXANDRO: I've got that raging headache again. Come over close to me, my dearest girl. (Maria *sits down on his lap; they kiss.*) I saw it again, as in a dream, like the Promised Land – a kind of tiny little sandy island and a mighty tree, and it seemed that you and I ...

MARIA: It must have been a chunk of Jamaica or the Bahamas. The Sales Office for the Tropical Islands plays tricks like that. Darling, you know how they try to influence you by telepathic means. Say, why don't we actually buy an archipelago somewhere?

ALEXANDRO: That's not what it was. (*Gets up.*) If you want an archipelago, we'll buy one. You know, Mary, I'm doing all these disgusting, nasty things and committing all these crimes solely for your sake. My love for you is quite unbelievable.

MARIA: Why do you call them nasty things, darling? What crimes? It's a perfectly normal job that will allow us to buy a nice archipelago. Don't torment me, darling!

ALEXANDRO: But do you love me?

MARIA: And how! One hundred and ten percent!

ALEXANDRO: If I became poor again, and was abandoned by all, and turned mean as hell, would you still love me?

MARIA: What sort of fantasy is that? Don't torment yourself, darling!

ALEXANDRO: (*Reciting Pasternak.*)

> To love another is a heavy cross,
> But you are lovely yet without device,
> And the secret of your charm is nothing less
> Than the key to the mystery of life.

MARIA: (*Hollowly.*) Don't torment me. Don't torment me, darling.

ALEXANDRO: (*Reciting Blok.*)

> Of valor and heroic deeds and fame
> On this pathetic earth I soon lost sight,
> When there before me in a simple frame
> Upon my writing desk your face shone bright.

MARIA: Don't torment me, I beg you ...

ALEXANDRO: (*Reciting Mayakovsky.*)

> I'll neither fling myself down flights of stairs,
> Or swallow poison,
> Nor could I ever put the gun against my temple.
> Apart from your gaze,
> There is no blade on any knife
> With power over me.

MARIA: Stop it, Alex, stop it! (*She gets up suddenly, totally transformed. Reciting Akhmatova.*)

Behind the hanging clouds of smoke, the voice
Of mournful violins begins to moan,
"Give heartfelt thanks to heaven and rejoice:
For once you have your loved one all alone."

ALEXANDRO: (*Emotionally. Reciting Pushkin.*)

My heart with rapture beats once more,
And inspiration from above,
And adoration as before,
Reborn – and life and tears and love!

MARIA: (*Decisively.*) Stop it. That's enough of that. Let's get this straight. Are we really such bleeding hearts? We've been reciting those Russian poets. Actually all you'll get from those Russians is trouble. That settles that, OK. We love each other and we'll buy an archipelago. Now, let's dance and quit talking, and then go over to some friends.

(Maria *turns on the television. An* Announcer *appears on the screen.*)

ANNOUNCER: Dear TV viewers! In our evening program, "Let's Talk About Love," a great friend and favorite of yours will put in a guest appearance. Undoubtedly you've already guessed who I'm talking about. Here he is: Pork Sausage.

(Pork *appears on the screen.*)

PORK SAUSAGE: Oh, tell me, what is love and why?
What makes it hopeless to define?
It is a feeling from on high
That tingles up and down your spine.

Let's talk about love, kids. Love, he-he-he, is a very serious matter. (*Takes a nip of whisky.*) Good, old boy Pork knows a lot about that stuff, don't you worry. Let's take unrequited love, for example. Let's suppose that you, Bobo, love Lola, but Lola, for example, doesn't love you. Bobo, as a real man and a patriot too, buys a bottle of Masculinus. Is he doing right? Yes, he's doing right, but not completely. Love, Bobo, is a delicate business and you won't get anywhere with only one bottle of our wonderful whisky. Right! Bobo figured the whole thing out, and in addition to the bottle of whisky he bought a bottle of port. By the way, port is produced by the Femininus Company, which is the Masculinus Company's sister branch. So Bobo goes over to Lola's house with a bottle of whisky and a bottle of port under each arm and says: "Lola, honey, look at that pretty birdie flying by the window." While Lola looks out the window, our Bobo mixes her a boilermaker. Lola drinks it down, her head begins to spin, and Bobo dumps her into bed. (*Takes a nip of whisky.*) That's how it's done, kids, go ahead, experiment. So long for now, I'm moving over to channel six.

MARIA: (*Turns the television off. Laughs.*) Did you absorb that advice?

ALEXANDRO: Yes, I did.

MARIA: Go ahead, experiment. After all, you made it up.

ALEXANDRO: Let's go.

MARIA: You don't have to experiment. I love you as it is. Will we buy an archipelago?

ALEXANDRO: Start the song.

MARIA: We're your soldiers, Masculinus

ALEXANDRO: (*Joins in.*) Masculinus, to battle lead us!

TOGETHER: Our rivals we'll obliterate,
All barriers eliminate!
Victorious thunder resound,
Masculinus expound!

(*They jump out through the window.*)

Curtain.

SCENE FOUR

In total darkness, the voices of the Stockholders, Alexandro, Miquelo, Gregoro *and* Maria *can be heard amplified through loudspeakers. A conference is taking place.*

MARIA: On the agenda for today: a brief survey of the situation in the country. The First Stockholder will address the meeting. You have the floor, Señor.

FIRST STOCKHOLDER: I shall begin with a few statistics. During the current month the daily demand for whisky per human specimen has increased from five hundred grams to one thousand five hundred grams, for a total increase of three hundred percent. During the same period the number of empty glass containers returned has decreased fifty percent. There is reason to suppose that the population, upon reaching the point of delirium, smashes the above mentioned empty glass containers which, it goes without saying, prompts increased production.

MARIA: Data concerning the Foreign and Internal Intelligence Agencies will be presented by the Second Stockholder. You have the floor, Señor.

SECOND STOCKHOLDER: I shall take the bull by the horns. In Africa business is picking up. The International Organization for Non-Alcoholic-Beverages has gone bankrupt. Trucks loaded with yoghurt have been intercepted everywhere. Within the country, numerous groups of young people, as well as members of the mass organization, The Young Bacchantes, are putting our ideas into action everywhere.

MARIA: Now the Third Stockholder will present the resume of our achievements. You have the floor, Señor.

THIRD STOCKHOLDER: Señores, in order to gauge the magnitude of our successes, it is fitting that we take a backward glance at the long road our firm has traveled. Let us go back to the very beginnings and remember our origins. Just a basement with the most primitive equipment: a few pots, and some homemade tubes – a mere handful of enthusiastic moonshiners. And what do we have now? Our present is dazzling, our future history is already being written by life itself! The idol of the nation, that wonderful Pork Sausage, the creation of our famous Advertising Department and above all Señor Alexandro, conquers more and more new minds for the glory of Masculinus! Bravo!

MARIA: The speeches are over. We'll open the meeting to discussion. Who wishes to speak? Señor Gregoro, you have the floor.

GREGORO: Under the leadership of the Council of the Stockholders, the musicians of our capital have achieved certain definite successes in the field of popularizing Masculinus products and principles. First place in those achievements goes to the songs: "We're Your Soldiers, Masculinus," "Masculinus – To Drink I'm Always Keen," "Tell Me, Little Birdie," and "Living Like Moles in Your Apartment Holes." At the same time I should like to point out a few shortcomings. The bassoons croak, the violins squeak, the saxophones bleat, the sounding boards and music stands have fallen to pieces, and mice have eaten up the scores. The music industry should be more generously financed.

MIQUELO: Now if you will allow me. Under the guidance and leadership and so on and so forth, the Fine Arts, true to the principles of Masculinus, have grown into an enormous force with which the barren altruists of the entire world have been compelled to reckon. At the same time it must be pointed out that our paint brushes are shedding their bristles, our easels have rotted away, our canvases are full of holes, and our paints have lost their colors. Hand over the cash! That's what we want!

ALEXANDRO: Under your inspired leadership and guidance, the Literary Guild of the Masculinus Company moves ever forward, achieving unheard of successes. It has long been common knowledge … Señor Stockholder Number One, stop pawing Maria!! Or I'll knock your block off!! It has long been common knowledge that our creation, Pork Sausage, has with lightning speed channeled all minds in the right direction. As an illustration, may I ask you to turn on your television sets, your telepathic systems, and other monitoring devices, and you will see how thoroughly Pork has entered into the life of our people. Turn on the equipment, Maria.

MARIA: Right away! Oh, Señor Stockholder Number One, take your hands off me! Alex, he's at me again!

ALEXANDRO: Now he's really going to get it right in the head!

(*A terrible fuss and racket can be heard.*)

FIRST STOCKHOLDER: Forgive me, Señor Alexandro, I couldn't help it. You know the way she walks. You know the way she swings her hips …

ALEXANDRO: Want some more?

FIRST STOCKHOLDER: No, that's enough, that's enough. Turn on the equipment, please.

(*Clicking of switches. One after the other various sources of light are turned on. At the rear of the stage, the facade of the main buildings of the Masculinus Company; in the windows, the* Stockholders, Maria, Alexandro, Gregoro *and* Miquelo. *Near the proscenium, there is a big outdoor coin-operated TV set with a motionless picture of* Pork Sausage *on the screen. At the proscenium there is a table at which sits a family, composed of* Bobo, Lola *and* Chiquito. *A* Blue-Collar Worker *stands holding a hammer in his hands; further back, three young maidens of enticing appearance with lutes poised on their knees – they are members of the Young* Bacchantes *Association; still further back behind the table, a* White-Collar Worker *sits holding a book by a green lamp. All three young people at the proscenium remain absolutely motionless in a tableau. A* Playboy *comes out on stage with a swaggering gait.)*

PLAYBOY: Is this ever boring – nothing going on here. What have you got to say about it, Pork? (*He puts a coin in the TV set. Immediately* Pork's *picture begins grimacing and winking, and from the bottom of the machine a bottle pops out. The* Playboy *opens the bottle, takes a swig.*)
PORK: Greetings to our golden youth! My famous ne'er-do-wells and Casanovas! What's the news from the sexual front?
PLAYBOY: As usual.
PORK: Feeling just a trifle bored, eh? Slight case of over-satiation?
PLAYBOY: Just a little bit.
PORK: Try going around on all fours.
PLAYBOY: (*Gets down on all fours.*) Like this?
PORK: Yeah, that's it!
PLAYBOY: Fabulous! Thanks, Pork! (*Goes out on all fours.*)
PORK: Well, kids, time to get move on.

(*The picture goes out. The people at the proscenium begin to move. The* Bacchantes *with innocent faces play their lutes softly. The* Blue-Collar Worker *hammers with his hammer. The* White-Collar Worker *turns the pages of his book.* Lola *pours coffee for* Chiquito. *With one hand* Bobo *strokes* Chiquito*'s head, with the other,* Lola*'s head. The Gershwin tune "You and I" is heard. The* Man of Independent Means *appears on stage, stops by the coin-operated TV set, and puts a coin in it.*)

MAN OF INDEPENDENT MEANS: What's up, Pork? How are things?
PORK: Nothing much.
MAN OF INDEPENDENT MEANS: (*Takes a nip of whisky, clinking the bottle with the TV set.*) So I play the six and he sits there swallowing flies. I cover the pot and he raises the ante.
PORK: There's no serious drinking or boozing it up with a guy like that.
MAN OF INDEPENDENT MEANS: You said it, Pork. You're a real brain, got a head on your shoulders. But what is there to do?
PORK: Try going around on all fours.
MAN OF INDEPENDENT MEANS: (*Gets down on all fours.*) Like this?
PORK: Yeah, that's it.
MAN OF INDEPENDENT MEANS: Terrific! Thanks, Pork. (*Goes out on all fours.*)

PORK: All right, get a move on, kids! Bobo! Lola! Chiquito! Girls! Come on now, girls! How about it, my beauties?

(*From above a gigantic bottle of Masculinus comes down with* Pork's *picture on the label. The lutes in the maiden's hands turn into bottles. The maidens start drinking.*)

LOLA: What was that you were singing before, Bobo?
BOBO: You and I, the two of us,
We'll build a nest …
LOLA: And how does Pork teach us to sing?
BOBO: You and I, the two of us
We'll pour a glass of Masculinus ...
CHIQUITO: The three of us, daddy, the three of us!
LOLA: The kid is right.
BOBO: The kid is right. From the mouth of babes. Pour some, Lola.
CHIQUITO: (*Fast.*) Mommy, let's drink to Daddy.
LOLA: (*Fast.*) To Daddy. (*They drink.*)
BOBO: (*Fast.*) Chiquito, let's drink to Mommy.
CHIQUITO: (*Fast.*) To Mommy. (*They drink.*)
LOLA: (*Fast.*) Bobo, let's drink to kiddy.
BOBO: (*Fast.*) To kiddy. (*They drink.*)
LOLA: To Lola baby. (*They drink.*)
CHIQUITO: To kiddy. (*They drink.*)
BOBO: To Bobo boy. (*They drink.*)
PORK: To all you kids. Good evening!
FAMILY: To our famous Pork! (*They drink.*)
BACCHANTES: Pork twist, everybody-body,
Pork, dance.
Superalcohol:
Pork, kissed, body-body-body!
Prance, dance.
Heads down, everybody-body!

(*They circle around the gigantic bottle in a Bacchante-like dance.*)

FIRST BACCHANTE: Shall we climb inside the bottle?
SECOND BACCHANTE: That's my dream – to sit right inside the bottle!
THIRD BACCHANTE: What bliss – to sit right inside the bottle!

(*They try to scramble up the bottle, but slide back down and fall.*)

PORK: Hey, all you gentlemen, why don't you help the girls?
BLUE-COLLAR WORKER: I'm busy creating material values.
WHITE-COLLAR WORKER: And I'm busy creating spiritual ones.
PORK: Aren't you ashamed? Smarter people than you have got over all that, and you're still playing the idiots.

BLUE-COLLAR WORKER: Sure, I'm ashamed, Pork.
WHITE-COLLAR WORKER: I'm suffering the worst sort of spiritual anguish, Señor Sausage, but I can't do a thing with myself.

(*Meanwhile* Bobo *has fallen under the table.* Chiquito *sits on top of it, and* Lola *staggers around it.*)

CHIQUITO: Daddy, my nose has already turned red, but yours is still white! How about it, sucker?
BOBO: Grr! Bow-wow! I'm in a terrific mood.
LOLA: Sonny boys, how many Mommies do you see?
CHIQUITO: I see three Mommies. Three whole Mommies!
LOLA: And I see five Sonny Boys.
BOBO: And I feel great. Bow! Wow!
FIRST BACCHANTE: (*Points at the* Blue-Collar Worker.) Look, what a nice satyr!
BLUE-COLLAR WORKER: I'm not a satyr, I'm a Blue-Collar Worker!
SECOND BACCHANTE: A marvellous specimen of a satyr!
THIRD BACCHANTE: He's not a satyr; he's a sheer delight!
FIRST BACCHANTE: Shall we swirl him in our Bacchante round-dance?
BLUE-COLLAR WORKER: Please, don't swirl me in your Bacchante round-dance.
SECOND AND THIRD BACCHANTES: We'll swirl the satyr round and round!

(*They swirl about in a Bacchante round-dance taking the* Blue-Collar Worker *with them.*)

WHITE-COLLAR WORKER: (*Lost in thought.*) The devil alone knows what's being created within me – a battle between good and evil. (*Continues his intellectual pursuits, but steals glances at the round-dance.*)
BOBO: (*Finally succeeds in pulling himself out from under the table, throws his arms around* Lola *and* Chiquito.) We're living better and better every day. Our life is so full-filling!
CHIQUITO: So full-fledged!
LOLA: So full-flowering!

(*They become lost in thoughts. They stagger.*)

BLUE-COLLAR WORKER: I'm exhausted.
BACCHANTES: Take a swig, satyr, take a swig! (*Forcibly stuffing the necks of their bottles into his mouth.*)
BOBO: So fully-fruitful!
CHIQUITO: So fully-furnished!
LOLA: So fully-flourishing!
BACCHANTES: Open the big bottle for us, satyr!

BLUE-COLLAR WORKER: That we can do. And with the greatest of pleasure. No problem, open and shut case. (*Drags the step-ladder up to the bottle and climbs up it.*)
BACCHANTES: There's a satyr for you! A genius of a satyr! Now we'll booze it up!

(*They go on with their dance.*)

CHIQUITO: When I was very little, I caught a cat!
BOBO: When I was very little, I caught a dog!
LOLA: When I was very little, I caught a horse!
BLUE-COLLAR WORKER: I don't know any theory, that's the whole trouble. Without a knowledge of theory, you can't open the bottle!
FIRST BACCHANTE: (*Points to the White-Collar Worker.*) Look at that darling little satyr sitting over there!

(*With a roar of laughter the* Bacchantes *encircle the* White-Collar Worker.)

WHITE-COLLAR WORKER: I'm not a satyr, I'm a White-Collar Worker.
SECOND BACCHANTE: What adorable little ears that satyr's got! (*Pulls his ears.*)
THIRD BACCHANTE: What cute little ribs that satyr's got! (*Tickles him.*)
FIRST BACCHANTE: Satyr, do you know any theory?
WHITE-COLLAR WORKER: He-he-he! As a matter of fact, I specialize in theory.
SECOND BACCHANTE: Open the bottle for us, dear, dear satyr! We want to booze it up! First of all, take a swig! There are a few drops left. Drink it all up! The last drops are always the sweetest!

(*They stuff their bottles into his mouth, then, dancing, lead him to the gigantic bottle, alongside of which the* Blue-Collar Worker *is standing on the step-ladder.*)

CHIQUITO: Shall we go on a binge?
BOBO: Lola, sharpen my knife.
LOLA: Hurrah! We're going on a binge! (*She sharpens his knife.*)
BLUE-COLLAR WORKER: Let's try some theory!
WHITE-COLLAR WORKER: Eeny meeny miney mo I don't know, eeny meeny miney mo, I do know.
BLUE-COLLAR WORKER: All done. (*Jumps down from the ladder and opens a tiny door in the side of the bottle.*) You can go in now. Who's first, the ladies, or you, as a member of the white-collar class?
WHITE-COLLAR WORKER: Please, dear Bacchantes, after you.
BACCHANTES: No, no, satyrs, the opening honors belong to you! Forward, satyrs!

(*They bicker about who'll go first.* Bobo *and the* Family *approach the bottle.*)

BOBO: (*Noticing the* White-Collar Worker.) I don't like four eyes! I'll stamp out four eyes!
CHIQUITO: He's our school-teacher.
BOBO: Ask him for his watch, kid.
CHIQUITO: (*Running over to the* White-Collar Worker.) Let me have your watch, Mister Teacher.
WHITE-COLLAR WORKER: (*Hysterically.*) No, no! I won't give it to you! You're always taking everything from me!
BOBO: (*Goes over to him.*) Give him your watch – the little boy is asking for it.
LOLA: No compassion for children? What a disgrace!
BOBO: No compassion, eh? No compassion? (*He kills the* White-Collar Worker *with one jab of his knife.*) Son-of-a-bitch of a theoretician!
BACCHANTES: (*Ecstatically.*) Some new companions! A great big satyr and a tiny little satyr! A pretty new Bacchante!
BLUE-COLLAR WORKER: (*Throws himself at* Bobo *with a loud yell.*) He killed a man! Help! Police!
BACCHANTES: Did he really kill someone? We didn't see anything! How annoying! One bottle-buddy less.
LOLA: That four eyes had no compassion for children!
CHIQUITO: He had no compassion for us!
BLUE-COLLAR WORKER: Help! Police! They killed a man!

(*At this moment* Pork Sausage *jumps out of the TV set.*)

PORK: (*Running across the stage.*) Let the man go, he's drunk! Can't you see he's drunk? (*Climbs back into the TV; from the screen.*) Well, kids, got a little rambunctious, did you; that's OK, could happen to anyone.
BACCHANTES: Could happen to anyone. Bacchanalian orgies don't come off without a few excesses. The man was drunk.
LOLA: Could happen to anyone. Bobo was drunk.
CHIQUITO: Could happen to anyone. Something like that could happen to anyone.

(*Taken aback, the* Blue-Collar Worker *lets go of* Bobo.)

BOBO: Cold-hearted snake! Got no compassion for a man when he's drunk!

(*With one jab of his knife, he kills the* Blue-Collar Worker.)

PORK: Oh, that's just terrific! And now try going around on all fours.

(*They all get down on all fours.*)

PORK: Now what do we need to do?
ALL TOGETHER: Booze it up! Booze it up!
PORK: Well then, climb into the bottle.

(*One after the other* Bobo, Lola, Chiquito *and the* Bacchantes *climb into the bottle. The light goes out. In total darkness* Alexandro *and* Maria *can be heard whispering.*)

ALEXANDRO: Mary, I'm all gooseflesh. I had the impression that Pork jumped right out of the TV set and ran across the stage. Did he really become materialized?

MARIA: It just seemed that way to you, darling. I didn't notice anything.

Curtain.

SCENE FIVE

Headquarters of the Advertising Department of the Masculinus Company. Alexandro *sits in an armchair, his hands covering his face. Enter* Miquelo *and* Gregoro.

MIQUELO: (*Coming in.*) It's a story simply bristling with allusions and hidden sexuality. This virgin named Snow White gets lost in the forest. From that point on, the two authors engage in total self-exposure …

GREGORO: A kind of moral strip-tease, eh? Not half bad. Go on.

MIQUELO: To make it brief, this nymphette … What's wrong with you, Alex?

GREGORO: Mary, what happened?

MARIA: Quiet, boys. Since last night's watching session, he's not been himself. All during the night he screamed about two murders, and about how some citizen, transformed by whisky into a beast, killed a professor and a worker with a knife. Did you notice anything like that? I didn't see anything of the sort.

GREGORO: Nonsense! What killings? The professor got drunk as a skunk and took a spill on the pavement.

MIQUELO: And the worker stiff drank himself into a horizontal position. There were three girl students there, they were the ringleaders.

GREGORO: And that family was something, remember Miq? Mom and Dad were just bursting with enthusiasm. They even let the little kid drink a shot.

MIQUELO: It was a very funny story. I was roaring with laughter on the inside, like a madman. But there weren't any killings.

MARIA: And all night long he muttered how everyone ended up climbing into some gigantic bottle.

GREGORO: That's a lot of tripe! It's quite simple, all those who could still stand on their feet went off to some bar. That was the end of the watching session.

MARIA: And Pork didn't jump out of the TV set, did he now, boys?

MIQUELO: Pork just kept gaping at everything peacefully with his tiny little eyes and only egged people on from time to time when somebody put a coin into the machine. How could a cartoon possibly jump out of the TV set?

MARIA: Hear that, Alex?

ALEXANDRO: I heard all that, and yet it all did happen, or could have happened, or will happen. Either Bobo killed them or he wanted to kill them, or he will kill them in the very near future …

MARIA: (*To her friends.*) In my opinion, he's starting to suffer from nightmares.

GREGORO: Shh! If the Council of Stockholders finds out about …

THUNDERING VOICE OF THE FIRST STOCKHOLDER: We already know about it! Señorita Maria, be so kind as to come to the main office.

ALEXANDRO: (*Jumping up.*) That Council of Stockholders can go kiss the devil's ass! Don't you dare go in there, Maria!

MIQUELO: Take it easy, Alex, sit down. (*Gets* Alexandro *to sit down.*) Let me tell you about this great little book I was reading yesterday, it'll give you a real laugh. This nymphette named Snow White gets lost in the forest and falls into a den of seven sex-fiends, who the authors, with a subtle sense of humor, depict as gnomes. Get it?

GREGORO: As far as I can understand, the two authors are heading straight for the edge of the abyss. A crystal-clear allegory like that …

ALEXANDRO: I'm afraid for you, my friends.

VOICE: Señorita Maria, come to the main office immediately.

ALEXANDRO: You can go to … ! Friends, I'm afraid for you; you're starting to degenerate in this cursed job. Everywhere you see hidden meanings of the cheapest sort, but you fail to notice the truly frightening aspects of other things going on behind the scenes.

VOICE: Señorita Maria, you are urgently summoned to the First Stockholder!

MARIA: What's got into him? I'll go find out.

ALEXANDRO: Can't you guess what's got into that impotent old goat? Innocent virtue, you simply can't guess. I'm terribly aftaid for you, Maria. You're liable to turn into a prostitute here.

VOICE: And you're not afraid for yourself, you schizophrenic?

ALEXANDRO: I'm afraid for myself. I may actually go out of my mind. I've committed a crime.

MARIA: What crime, darling? What are you raving about?

ALEXANDRO: And what about Pork Sausage – isn't that a crime? My monster, Pork Sausage, the personification of all alcoholic virtues ... Basta, I'm saying good-bye to cynicism, I won't be a toady to this diabolical company any longer. While it's still not too late, I'll do away with Pork!

MARIA: How can you do that?

ALEXANDRO: I fathered him and I'll kill him too! Ha-ha, it's quite simple – I won't write any more speeches for him, and I'll leave the company, and that'll be the end of it. Pork will fade from view, he'll melt away like a bad dream. Maria, wave "bye-bye," we're leaving. (*Takes* Maria *by the hand.*)

MIQUELO and GREGORO: And what about us?

ALEXANDRO: You leave too. We'll devote ourselves to creative work, we'll create and we'll sleep peacefully, and in our dreams we'll see a tiny little sandy island with one single palm tree all by itself, gigantic and generous. The Freedom Tree.

MIQUELO: Well, what do you say, Gregoro, will be able to renounce the old world?

GREGORO: Sure, we'll shake the dust off our feet!

MARIA: (*Aggrieved.*) Darling, does that mean that we won't buy an archipelago? Only dream about some wretched little island, is that it?

ALEXANDRO: First thing we do, we'll buy ourselves an archipelago, a reliable, suitably remote archipelago. And boys, I advise you to do the same – buy yourselves each at least one small archipelago per person.

MARIA: Terrific! Then let's go! It's just great, I'll be the owner of an archipelago!

GREGORO: Miq, shall we buy one archipelago for the two of us?

MIQUELO: Better make it two separate ones, or otherwise we'll fight. Separate, but near-by.

(*Suddenly a weak humming can be heard. The TV set has turned on all by itself.*)

ANNOUNCER: (*Smiling.*) The Pork Sausage "Home and Family Show."

PORK: Listen, kids, I've heard that Lola decided to buy her family that clever new appliance – the combination floor-polisher and juice-maker with dish-washer and chamber pot attached. She did absolutely the right thing: Lola's a dear girl, a brainy little half-wit. Of course, life should be made easier, but look here, kids, you shouldn't forget the best interests of our beloved comp ...

(*Suddenly* Pork Sausage *freezes with his mouth wide open. The dumbfounded face of the* Announcer *flashes for a moment.*)

VOICE: What's the matter, Señor Alexandro, is something wrong with the telepathic transmitter?

ALEXANDRO: See? Basta, the end of Pork, bad luck take him. We're off!

MARIA: Forward, to our archipelago!

(*They all go out. The constrained whispering of the* Stockholders *can be heard.*)

THIRD STOCKHOLDER: Our youngsters have left. What are we going to do? (*Sobs.*)

SECOND STOCKHOLDER: I'll get in touch with Ambrosio right this minute. He'll show them, damn it!

FIRST STOCKHOLDER: Easy. Don't become carried away. Don't get into a panic, dear brothers-in-arms.

ANNOUNCER: Due to technical difficulties, the "Home and Family Show" will not be shown at this time. Instead, we shall broadcast a program for our small friends. (*Sings.*)

Tell me, little birdie,
What do you buy ? ...

Curtain.

SCENE SIX

On stage, a small contemporary apartment, divided into rooms by thin partition walls: kitchen, bathroom, dining room, and study in which Alexandro *is sitting at a desk writing and at the same time delivering a monologue.*

ALEXANDRO: My friend, life here on these far-off archipelagos, although it may be monotonous, is not without its own distinctive charm, and I would not change it for any other. This simple, healthy life far removed from the vanities of the mainland opens up broad perspectives for reflection and self-perfection. We have neither radio nor television, we receive no newspapers and, could you imagine, we don't miss any of that. Contact with the great minds and lofty souls of the past provides Maria and me with true delight and happiness. I work a great deal, and in the evenings we read aloud the poets of a certain country, which is well known to you.

(Maria *appears. She walks across the kitchen wearing a bathrobe, then disappears into the bathroom, and turns the water on. The sound of running water can be heard.*)

ALEXANDRO: Do you hear the roar of the sea, my friend? Our archipelago is surrounded on all sides by hissing, snow-white ocean spray. Maria is a hardy swimmer; every day she spends ten hours in the ocean. Our only ties to the outer worlds are those small launches which bring provisions once a week. I shall dispatch this letter to you by means of one of them. I am writing to you, not because I want you to furnish me with news about the latest paroxysms of that cursed civilization of yours, but because I wish to establish a deep and vital spiritual contact with you. In our century of convulsive telephone calls and stereotyped telegrams, let us, my friend, revive the noble epistolary genre for which the past century was so justly famous. (*Becomes lost in thoughts.*)

(*A ring and knock at the door. Slipping on her bathrobe,* Maria *opens the door. Enter a* Delivery Man *in green overalls and dark glasses.*)

DELIVERY MAN: Ma'am, I have your vegetables for you. Turnips, tomatoes, celery. (*Hands her a bag.*)

MARIA: Thanks, I'll bring the money right away. (*Runs to the kitchen and back, and gives him the money.*) Keep the change.

DELIVERY MAN: (*Insinuatingly.*) Ma'am your bathrobe got wet at the bottom.

MARIA: (*With a laugh.*) I just jumped out of the tub.

DELIVERY MAN: (*In a high, sing-song tone of voice.*) Ma'am, your bathrobe comes down to the floor. Nowadays they are not wearing that kind any more.

MARIA: That's ridiculous. I bought this robe at "Elegantina's."

DELIVERY MAN: Ma'am, you're living almost in the center of town, but you just don't understand. Now long bathrobes have been replaced by short jackets. They come down only to about here. (*Tries to show where on* Maria*'s body.*)

MARIA: (*Pushing him away.*) Have you gone crazy?

DELIVERY MAN: Sorry, ma'am. I'm only a delivery man. (*Goes out.*)

MARIA: (*Laughing.*) Wonder of wonders!

(*A ring and knock at the door. The same* Delivery Man *comes in again, but this time in red overalls.*)

DELIVERY MAN: Ma'am, I have some bologna for you.

MARIA: Thanks, I'll bring the money right away. (*Runs to the kitchen and back, and gives him the money.*) Keep the change.

DELIVERY MAN: (*Distressed.*) Phew, Ma'am, that's an outrageously long bathrobe you are wearing. Tut-tut-tut!

MARIA: Don't be a boor!

DELIVERY MAN: Excuse me, Ma'am, you should accentuate your figure, not wrap it up in some Roman toga. Your figure is not just your own personal property, it's in the public domain. Beauty belongs to everyone.

MARIA: (*Mockingly, but all the same unintentionally coquettish.*) To everyone? Even to a wretched little delivery man bringing bologna?

DELIVERY MAN: Tell me, what have you got against delivery men bringing bologna? Look at how graceful I am! (*He executes a few rhythmic ballet-like steps.*)

MARIA: (*Automatically imitates his movements, then recollecting herself.*) I don't want to know anyone else except my husband!

DELIVERY MAN: (*Crudely.*) To hell with that husband of yours, that bookworm. Here you live almost in the very center of town, and yet you think like a savage on a desert island!

MARIA: (*Opening the door.*) Down the stairs merrily you go!

DELIVERY MAN: My warmest regards, Ma'am! (*Leaves.*)

MARIA: (*Closing the door.*) These delivery men are getting fresher and fresher by the day!

(*A ring and a knock at the door. The same* Delivery Man *comes in again, this time in white overalls.*)

DELIVERY MAN: Ma'am, I have some milk and cream for you.
MARIA: Thanks, I'll bring the money right away. (*Runs to the kitchen and back and gives him the money.*) Keep the change.
DELIVERY MAN: Ma'am, what an elegant bathrobe you're wearing! What exquisite taste!
MARIA: (*Pleased.*) Do you really think so?
DELIVERY MAN: What a light step you have, and your voice jingles like the change in your hand.
MARIA: (*Mockingly.*) Delivery men have begun to speak like poets.
DELIVERY MAN: I'm not a delivery man.
MARIA: Who are you, then?
DELIVERY MAN: I am an adventurer. (Maria *is intrigued. The* Delivery Man *takes out his pocket-radio and turns it on.*) May I ask you for a dance?

(*Spins* Maria *around with much ceremony.*)

MARIA: I haven't danced for such a long time! So you're not a delivery man?
DELIVERY MAN: I am a real he-man. My specialty is forgery and black marketeering, I have amassed a sizable fortune, and besides that, I am a music lover and an Anglophile.
MARIA: You are a man-of-the-world. What's new downtown?

(*They dance. The* Delivery Man *whispers something in her ear.* Maria *laughs.*)

ALEXANDRO: All my past life, my friend, now seems to me to be a bad dream. I have the feeling that I went astray; I have the feeling that I did despicable things. Basta, I have come to my senses, and now in my far-off archipelago I have finally started to live, to think, to feel, to love. And so I embrace you and await your answer. Your Alexandro. (*Gets up and seals the envelope.*)
DELIVERY MAN: Does your bathrobe have buttons or a zipper?
MARIA: (*Laughing.*) That's my little secret. A company secret.

(Alexandro *enters with the letter in his hand.* Maria *and the* Delivery Man *stop dancing.*)

ALEXANDRO: (*To the* Delivery Man.) Are you from the boat?
DELIVERY MAN: I deliver the milk, Señor. (*He winks to* Maria.)
MARIA: Yes, that's right, darling, he's from the boat.
ALEXANDRO: Would you be so kind as to deliver my letter to the mainland?
DELIVERY MAN: To the mainland, Señor?

MARIA: Just drop it in the mailbox on the corner. He'll be so kind, darling.
DELIVERY MAN: Your humble servant. Good-bye, Ma'am! (*Leaves.*)
ALEXANDRO: So it seems you did a little dancing with that sailor, eh?
MARIA: Yes, I did. He asked me how my bathrobe fastens.
ALEXANDRO: That's a strange question for a sailor to ask.
MARIA: (*Sharply.*) Stop pretending! I'm sick and tired of this. I'm sick and tired of living in total isolation.
ALEXANDRO: Are you sick and tired of our archipelago?
MARIA: I'm sick and tired of this hole! We live almost in the very center of town and yet we see nothing, we go nowhere. I want to go to the movies, to a burlesque show, to a nightclub. I want to drink, damn it all!
ALEXANDRO: What's wrong with you, dearest? We've been so happy. Let's drink our milk and read Flaubert. (*Hands Maria a bottle of milk, takes a mouthful himself from another.*) My God! It's whisky! (*Flings the bottle away.*) That bestial smell of Masculinus! Shit! What infamy! What a cesspool!
MARIA: (*Takes a swig of whisky.*) It actually is whisky! Hurrah! It's whisky! Now I'll get a snootful! Good, old Masculinus! Darling, remember when we worked for Masculinus? We were the Kings of Life then! Remember what a swell life that was?
ALEXANDRO: We were nothing but slaves and criminals, criminal slaves! Get a hold of yourself, Mary!

(Maria *weaves about. A ring and a knock at the door. Enter the same* Delivery Man, *but this time in yellow overalls.*)

DELIVERY MAN: Ma'am I have newspapers for you. (*Hands* Maria *a bundle of newspapers.*)
ALEXANDRO: What sort of impudence is this? I have expressly forbidden the boats of the yellow press to draw near my shores! Throw that trash away! (*Grabs the newspapers away from* Maria *and flings them to the floor, then turns to the* Delivery Man.) Who are you?
DELIVERY MAN: I am a newspaper delivery man and a gentleman. I do not allow women to be insulted in my presence. Especially not a woman like this, the pride of our country. (*He picks up the newspapers and hands them to* Maria.)
MARIA: (*Grabs the newspapers.*) Hurrah! The daily bulletin from "The Young Bacchantes"! My creation is still alive! (*Glances feverishly through the newspapers.*) Look, how short skirts have become! What décolletage! What terse slogans! We've gotten so far behind the times, Alexandro!
ALEXANDRO: (*Carefully looking the* Delivery Man *over.*) You're no newspaper delivery man.
DELIVERY MAN: I am a real he-man.
ALEXANDRO: Come into my study. (*Goes first.*)

DELIVERY MAN: Gladly, Señor. (*Whispers to* Maria.) Get all dressed up, Ma'am. Shorten your skirts, deepen your décolletage. I am inviting you to a nightclub.
MARIA: It's a deal, you're on! Long live civilization!

(Maria *runs out. The* Delivery Man *goes into* Alexandro*'s study and sits down on the desk.*)

DELIVERY MAN: (*Looks around the study, laughing and sneering at* Alexandro.) The Holy of Holies? The Ivory Tower? The mysterious archipelago? That means that it was here (*Pulls the letter out of his pocket*), far removed from the vanities of the mainland, that you rubbed shoulders with the great minds and lofty souls of the past?
ALEXANDRO: (*In a rage.*) Where did you get my letter from, you scoundrel? (*Tries to grab the letter away from him.*)
DELIVERY MAN: (*Jumping away.*) And during the evenings you read aloud the poets of a certain well-known country, whose name we won't mention. I wonder what country that might be? Could it be Rus ... ?

(*Draws menacingly near.*)

ALEXANDRO: You scum, do you think I'm a puny little intellectual? Do you think I can't deal with you? (*Grabs the* Delivery Man *by the shirtfront.*)
DELIVERY MAN: (*Falling on his knees.*) Daddy, don't destroy me! Daddy, take pity on me! Won't you show any mercy for your own child? Father! Flesh of my flesh!
ALEXANDRO: (*Disconcerted, lets go of him.*) Loony! Madman! Why do you call me your father?
DELIVERY MAN: (*Giggling.*) Child-murderer! Don't you recognize your own offspring? Stop this masquerade. I'm Pork Sausage. (*Takes off his overalls and dark glasses, sticks on a moustache, pulls a funny little hat out of thin air and slaps it on the back of his head, and lo and behold, there before our very eyes,* Pork Sausage *appears.*) Greetings, Pop! (*Throws his arms around* Alexandro.) No, no, it's not a dream! Want me to pinch you? (*Pinches him.*) Well, how about it, are you finally convinced, Pop?
ALEXANDRO: (*Pushing* Pork *away.*) It still is a dream, a case of pure delirium! It's nothing but a masquerade, a childish trick on the part of Masculinus. (*Takes a few steps back, looks at him.* Pork *sits on the desk, twisting his moustache and doffing his cap as a greeting.*) Listen Pork, I killed you a long time ago. I fathered you, and I killed you. Why are you trying to get me all mixed up?
PORK: (*Playfully wags his finger at him.*) Oh, Papa, you're the crafty one, trying to get out of paying alimony! (*Suddenly starts to sob.*) Bad Papa, left his poor baby all alone to the mercy of fate. I truly loved you so much,

worshipped you, I recited in such a state of ecstasy all those not so successful speeches of yours. (*He wipes his tears away and smiles*.) Peekaboo, Pater, now I've got better authors than you – tough guys who aren't slobbering all the time. Now we influence our citizens through absolute indoctrination.

ALEXANDRO: (*Gloomily*.) What does that mean?

PORK: Go out on the street, pussycat, and see for yourself.

ALEXANDRO: What do you want from me, revolting Señor Sausage?

PORK: Not very much at all. In the first place: to destroy this so-called ivory tower of yours. Isolation of this kind won't bring you any good, my friend. In the second place: to do away with your spiritual independence and inspire you with the life-giving spirit of cynicism, in other words, to destroy your personality. In the third place: to corrupt your charming wife.

ALEXANDRO: And what else do you want, you hideous creature? (*Hurls himself at* Pork.)

PORK: (*Runs off with a laugh*.) I want to go pee-pee, Pop!

ALEXANDRO: (*Chasing him*.) Maybe you want to be six feet under pushing up daisies, you cur?

PORK: (*Jumping up on top of the table*.) I want to go poo-poo, Pop!

ALEXANDRO: Maybe you want to be thrown off a cliff, head first?

PORK: (*Jumping up on the lamp, rocking back and forth*.) I want wa-wa, Pop!

ALEXANDRO: What else do you want, you snake? (*Jumping up to grab him*.)

PORK: (*Jumps on the sofa, running off just out of* Alexandro*'s reach and singing in a mocking fashion*.) Living like moles, in your small apartment holes, pop a cork, drink along with Pork … Pappy, Pappy, got all tired out, poor little sappy?

ALEXANDRO: And what if I hit you in the head with this heavy object? (*Throws the desk lamp at* Pork.)

PORK: (*Jumping aside*.) Now, is that nice to throw a desk lamp at the idol of the nation?

ALEXANDRO: Then I'll throw a chair at the idol of the nation! (*Throws the chair at* Pork.)

PORK: (*Jumping aside*.) It's not nice, it's very nasty, and what about morality? And what about humanism? And non-resistance to evil?

ALEXANDRO: Paperweight to the snout! (Alexandro *throws the paperweight at* Pork.)

PORK: (*Jumping aside*.) There's nothing more frightful than an intellectual who's gone berserk! No reflexes for self-control! Monster! Pithecanthropus! And that's my father! Oh, you literary men, you literary men, there's no way of getting you to listen to reason!

ALEXANDRO: I'll smash your head with this wastebasket! All my unrealized dreams right at your belly! (*Throws the wastebasket at* Pork.)

PORK: (*Jumping aside.*) Please tell us – what are you working on these days?

ALEXANDRO: Shakespeare to the temple! Greatness and nobility right at the forehead! (*Throws a large volume containing Shakespeare's complete works at* Pork.)

PORK: (*Jumping aside.*) Dear TV viewers, we dropped in on the well-known writer Señor Alexandro in his study ...

ALEXANDRO: The Divine Comedy to the rib-cage! (*Throws a large volume at Pork.*)

PORK: (*Jumping aside.*) We put the following question to him, "What are you working on these days?" "I'm familiarizing myself with the heritage of the classics," he answered, and threw a volume of Dante at us: You should remember, Daddy, that thanks to this little button all your acts of vandalism are being filmed for the evening news.

ALEXANDRO: Being filmed? So much the better! Now before the eyes of the whole world, I'll riddle you with bullets. (*Pulls out a revolver and takes aim.*)

PORK: (*Jumping up on the windowsill, flings the window open.*) Boys, my-old-man-tormentor wants to take my life! Boys, my old-man-tormentor's got a fire-arm!

(*Outside the window the savage roar of the crowd bursts forth.* Pork *jumps out of the window. Throwing his revolver away,* Alexandro *collapses on the sofa and sobs in despair. At just this moment* Pork *appears in the entrance hall where* Maria *comes out dressed in more than risque fashion.*)

PORK: (*Takes* Maria *by the arm and leads her to the door. Singing the first lines of Vertinsky's romance.*)

> In evening restaurants
> In café-chantants,
> In cheap electric paradise ...

MARIA: Shall we take my spouse along?

PORK: (*With gallantry.*) Dear lady, your spouse caught diarrhea from a mouse!

MARIA: Ha-ha-ha, ha-ha-ha, my spouse caught diarrhea from a mouse! Witty, witty! My beloved spouse sat down in the outhouse. Not bad either, is it? But you're not married, are you, Señor? It's so nice that you're not married. It's a great rarity these days. My spouse caught diarrhea from a mouse. Ha-ha-ha!

PORK: Your beloved spouse sat down in the outhouse. Ha-ha-ha! (*They go out.*)

ALEXANDRO: (*Gets up.*) So the worst imaginable has actually come to pass – Pork has materialized. I did not succeed in destroying him. Some course of action must be taken. The battle must be joined. I'll go to my friends, to

Gregoro, to Miquelo. Together, the three of us will be able to defeat that monster. We shall see, Pork, we shall see! You've succeeded in one thing – you've destroyed my ivory tower. My archipelago doesn't exist anymore. My apartment is here in the very center of town surrounded by raging alcoholic crowds. Forward! To the people! To sow the seeds of the rational, the good, and the eternal! (*Passes through the entire apartment, and at the door bumps into the* General.)

GENERAL: (*Standing at attention saluting.*) Do I have the honor of greeting that great master of contemporary fiction, Señor Alexandro?

ALEXANDRO: I'm Alexandro.

GENERAL: Very glad to meet you. I am a General in the Rocket Cavalry, doubling as a doorman at the Department of Social Harmony.

ALEXANDRO: What can I do for you, General?

GENERAL: I serve you this summon to appear at the Department of Social Harmony. Tomorrow, at the specified time, you are to come straight to the Director himself. I assure you, our Director has a lucid intellect and an enlightened mind of vast dimensions. (*Shows the dimensions with his hands.*) A personal meeting with him is sheer pleasure, like a rendezvous with a lady or ... hmm ... with a mare. Attendance is compulsory. Failure to appear means cutting off the earlobes. Hasta la vista!

(*Disappears.*)

Curtain.

SCENE SEVEN

The stage is divided into two parts – a waiting room and the office of the Director of the Department of Social Harmony. In the office there is huge table with many telephones and a switchboard. In addition, there are several large bottles of Masculinus whisky standing on the table. A special chair equipped with an enormous symbolic coil. Portraits of the three Stockholders *with children on their laps hang on the walls. Above them, a portrait of* Pork Sausage. *Above* Pork*'s portrait, the slogan, "Masculinus – it's the Maximum!" The office is connected to the waiting room by a door. In addition to this door, the waiting room has three other doors. A buffet with food and liquor stands in the corner. Still life paintings on various Masculinus themes hang on the walls, as well as the slogan, "Art workers, delve deeper into the heart of your subject."*

The General *stands behind the buffet drying glasses. Enter* Gregoro *looking around.*

GENERAL: Just one moment, Señor Gregoro. Stand at attention, look straight at me. Chin up, that's it. (*Takes* Gregoro*'s picture.*) Thank you. Won't you take some refreshment? (*Hands* Gregoro *a hot dog.*)
GREGORO: Thanks.
GENERAL: Don't mention it, it's just a trifle! Please sign for it in the register.

(Gregoro *signs his name and goes to the proscenium with his refreshment.*)

GENERAL: How do you like your hot dog, Señor Gregoro?
GREGORO: A most unusual hot dog, General. It brings back memories of childhood.
GENERAL: Right you are. All the hot dogs we serve are like that. Special reserve.

(*Enter* Miquelo.)

GENERAL: Stand at attention, Señor Miquelo. Chin up. Look straight at me. (*Takes his picture.*) Thank you. Take some refreshment. (*Hands* Miquelo *a hot dog.*) Sign here.
MIQUELO: (*Goes over to* Gregoro.) Greetings, Gregoro. What an amazing hot dog. You know, I took a bite and suddenly I remembered my childhood.

GREGORO: I'm completely under the spell of childhood memories too.

(*Enter* Alexandro.)

GENERAL: (*Runs out from behind the buffet with his camera.*) Saluto, saluto, Señor Alexandro! Be so kind as to stand at attention! Brush back that unruly lock of hair ftom your forehead! More optimism in your look, more life! Why such gloom! Chin up! Say honeydew. Look this way, watch the birdie! That's it. (*Takes* Alexandro*'s picture.*) Thank you. Take some refreshment. Sign the book.

ALEXANDRO: (*Goes over to his friends.*) Greetings, boys. What an amazing hot dog. Only when we were children were there such delicious hot dogs.

GREGORO: (*Proudly.*) It's from special reserve. They're treating us to special reserve.

MIQUELO: Best of all – it's on the house. You sign the register and get refreshments free. Wonder of wonders!

ALEXANDRO: And our childhood, our childhood – that's best of all. The smells of our golden childhood.

(*They stand lost in thoughts with their hot dogs in their mouths.*)

GENERAL: (*Sings as he dries glasses.*)

> Now I remember the battles of yore,
> When the whole earth started to sway,
> And all the bullet wounds and gore,
> The shell shock, with hi-ho and hey-hey.
> You come out alive upon a hill,
> But before a single word can be said,
> Some fragment of a bursting shell
> Detaches your shoulders from your head.

(*It should be said that during all this time various busy preparations are going on in the* Director*'s office. Every now and then* Maria *– wearing a cat-mask – goes back and forth, her heels clicking on the floor in a business-like fashion. She straightens something on the table, picks up the telephone receivers, writes down something.* Feodoro *– in a donkey-mask – with a very scholarly air settles down in the corner behind a small, separate table and opens a thick ledger. Three attendants in uniforms and wolf-masks move chairs about, drag in some wires, plug them in somewhere, and then hide behind a curtain so that only their shoes are visible. The* Director *of the Department – in a jacket and a goat-mask – appears and sits down in the special chair.* Maria *sticks a pipe attached to the coil into his mouth. The* Director *sucks on the pipe and thumbs through some papers. Lights flash on the switchboard.*)

ALEXANDRO: (*Taking the hot dog out of his mouth.*) Well, how about it friends, are you sowing the seeds of the rational, the good, and the eternal?

MIQUELO: I was just about to start sowing, but then there's this party with free hot dogs …

GREGORO: … hot dogs from special reserve. Exactly what's going on I couldn't tell you. Maybe a major policy change is in the works?

ALEXANDRO: Really, these hot dogs are leading us totally astray. We've got to be on our guard, friends. To hell with these hot dogs. Let's throw them away. (*He throws his hot dog away.*)

MIQUELO: That's right! To hell with them! (*Makes a gesture as if to throw his hot dog away, but surreptitiously conceals it in his pocket.*)

GREGORO: That's right! What are we doing standing here with hot dogs in our mouths? (*Carefully wraps his hot dog in his handkerchief and puts it in his pocket.*)

GENERAL: Cigars, gentlemen?

(Miquelo *is the first to dash over to get his cigar,* Gregoro *follows him, and then* Alexandro *goes, too. All three get a cigar each and sign in the register. They stand silently with their cigars in their mouths.* Maria *appears in the waiting room with a list in her hand.*)

MARIA: Señor musician, dear maestro Gregoro, this way please! (*Goes out.*)

ALEXANDRO: Remember, Gregoro, no giving, in.

MIQUELO: Be firm, old boy.

(Gregoro *enters the office. The* Director *gets up to meet him, politely showing him the chair.* Gregoro *sits down. Behind his back and without noticing it, the* Attendants *plug in some plugs and hide behind the curtain again. The* Director *makes a sign to* Feodoro. Feodoro *opens his ledger. The conversation begins.*)

GENERAL: Yes indeed, I've seen you come and go, Señores artistas. So many of your brothers have passed before my eyes. On certain days we handle up to fifty souls. Sometimes it simply makes you cry. Such beautiful individuals.

MIQUELO: What are you crying for, Pop?

GENERAL: Oh, just because ...

ALEXANDRO: As a general rule, old warriors tend to be sentimental.

GENERAL: That's exactly it! You know, I've taken part in so many battles, and I'm a drinking man too, but somehow I still can't get used to the sight of corpses.

(*At this moment the conversation in the office draws to a close.* Gregoro *falls out of the chair to the floor. The* Attendants *carry his body out. The* Director *presses a button.* Maria *appears and passes through the office to the waiting room.*)

MARIA: Señor painter, dear maestro Miquelo, this way please! (*Goes out.*)

MIQUELO: But where's Gregoro?

GENERAL: (*Cheering up, sings.*) But where's our Gregoro, our little Gregoro, oh, where did he fly away to?

ALEXANDRO: Be on your guard, old boy ...

MIQUELO: I will. (*Enters the office. Exactly what happened to* Gregoro *is repeated with* Miquelo.)

ALEXANDRO: (*Goes over to the buffet.*) Why are you wearing a general's uniform, what kind of a stupid theatrical prop is that? What kind of a General are you, if you're just an ordinary bartender-flunkey?

GENERAL: (*In a voice trembling with righteous indignation.*) Señor, your youth does not give you the right to ridicule an old soldier! Before you stands a real General who has earned his rank by fighting for his country, which includes you too, disrespectful young man.

ALEXANDRO: A General on the retired list?

GENERAL: I shall never go on the retired list. I am a real General in the Rocket Cavalry.

ALEXANDRO: Does our country really have rockets?

GENERAL: Ha-ha-ha! Compared to us, Russia and America are mere pygmies. We have the most powerful rocket cavalry in the entire world. The most mobile and the most invulnerable. I am about to enlighten you, Señor Alexandro. I can let you in on a military secret; now you won't be able to blab.

ALEXANDRO: What does it mean, "now you won't be able to?"

GENERAL: (*Changing the subject.*) Well, you're a patriot, aren't you?

ALEXANDRO: Yes, but why that "now"?

GENERAL: Well, now you're a patriot, aren't you?

ALEXANDRO: I've always been a patriot, and not just now.

GENERAL: You've always been a patriot, that's exactly what I meant. To make a long story short, following my suggestion, the army has been completely restructured. Gone forever are all complicated technical devices, interception stations, tracking stations, etc., etc. All that is sheer nonsense, Señor Alexandro, just one more target for the enemy. Now our rockets are placed on the backs of horses, on wild mares dispersed over the boundless expanses of our vast pampas. Ha-ha-ha, a clever move, eh, Señor? Just let the enemy try to strike at countless herds of wild mares! It will be a futile gesture, I can assure you.

ALEXANDRO: How long have you been drinking, General?

GENERAL: (*Proudly.*) Since earliest childhood I have felt a strong attraction to alcohol, and now under the leadership of Masculinus I won't ever sober up.

(Miquelo *falls out of the chair to the floor. They carry his body out.* Maria *passes through the office and goes to the waiting room.*)

MARIA: Señor writer, dear master of the art of fiction, Alexandro, your presence is requested in the office! (*Goes out.*)

ALEXANDRO: That's odd, where's Miquelo?

GENERAL: (*Cheering up.*) But where's Miquelo, our nice little Miquelo, poor, poor little Miquelo, oh, where has he flown away to? (*Cries.*)

(Alexandro *enters the office. he is received exactly the same way as his friends. The conversation begins.*)

GENERAL: (*Crying quietly.*) Such fine artists ... beautiful individuals ... I still can't get used to the sight of corpses ... even one's own corpse is frightening sometimes ... (*He turns off the lights above the buffet, sweeps the room, stops in front of the mirror and looks at his own reflection, then runs off with a cry of horror.*)

DIRECTOR: Now look here, my dear Señor Alexandro, why the dinking dink, don't our young writers ever write anything about love, the dinked-up dinkers? About pure dinking love, dink them all, the dinkers? Dink it, it's all one big obscenity! You understand me, Señor Alexandro? I'm no narrow-minded prude, but just where are our Romeos and Juliets, dink it all, up their dinking dinked-off dinkers?

ALEXANDRO: You can't be aware of the latest developments, you can't have read the right things, there's a lot of good writing about love being done in this country, but none of it gets published, and instead they publish filthy books steeped in alcohol and debauchery.

DIRECTOR: That's right. That's just what I'm saying – why don't our young writers write even one dinking little word about love? You see, I went out to some dinking little small town, and got together some five or six crummy people for some dinking, dinked-up meeting. There's this Dante, what do you call him, Alighieri or some other slug-a-fug. So I say, what's wrong with you, Señor Alighieri, you don't even write one dinking little word about pure, dinking, ideal love? And he answers me back – I don't write on orders, he says. Did you get that, Alex? Did you get what he's pulling, that dinking dinked-up Alighieri?

ALEXANDRO: Who told you you could call me Alex, Señor Director? I didn't think we were on such intimate terms?

DIRECTOR: (*Hurt.*) You're always like that, you dinking artists, you turn your backs on us here at the Department. We do this, we do that for you, and all you do is show us your rear-ends. Don't get in a huff, Señor Alexandro, no need to go on the defensive, we're all on the same side. Don't think we're just pen-pushers here. We can even have a drink with an artist. Listen, Alex, if you like, I can put the pipe from my own personal apparatus into your mouth. I never offered it to anyone else before, but I'm offering it to you now.

ALEXANDRO: There's Masculinus in the apparatus, right?
DIRECTOR: The purest, the most aromatic Masculinus.
ALEXANDRO: I don't drink Masculinus.

(*A pause.*)

DIRECTOR: Is that so?
ALEXANDRO: Yes, that's so!
DIRECTOR: Is that so?
ALEXANDRO: Yes, that's so!
DIRECTOR: Well, then, that's so. But maybe, if you're interested, Alex, I can fix you up with something, how about it? Our country, needless to say, isn't just flowing with milk and honey, but we can find something, understand? (*Rubs his thumb and forefinger together in front of* Alexandro*'s nose.*) Interested, Alex?

(*A pause.*)

DIRECTOR: (*Turns on the switchboard.*) Interested, Alex?

(*A pause. The switchboard emits a growing wail.*)

DIRECTOR: Interested, Alex?
ALEXANDRO: Don't you dare call me Alex!

(*The telephone rings.*)

DIRECTOR: (*Picks up the receiver.*) Yes. Yes. Let him go dip his dinking dink! (*Hangs up the receiver.*) Interested, or not interested, Alex?
ALEXANDRO: Not interested! What right do you have to get so familiar with me? We hardly know each other.
DIRECTOR: (*Turns the switchboard off.*) My dear man, where did you ever get the idea that we hardly know each other? Take a closer look. (*Takes off his goat-mask.*)
ALEXANDRO: (*In horror.*) Pork Sausage!
PORK: (*Roars with laughter.*) What a great meeting! Hi, Daddy! You fathered me, but I'll kill you. Get it? (*Claps his hands.*) Everyone in here!

(Maria *comes into the office.* Feodoro *gets up from behind the table, the Attendants come out from behind the curtain.*)

PORK: Masks off everyone!

(*They all take off their masks.*)

ALEXANDRO: So it's you, Feodoro? My friend, how on earth did you get into this den of thieves?
FEODORO: (*In confusion.*) I didn't even realize it was me. But I don't really

do anything here, Alexandro. I'm just a small cog in the machine, I only register the executions. I ...

ALEXANDRO: Maria? Is it you? My sweetheart? Here?

MARIA: I didn't realize it was me! Alex, darling, I'm only the secretary. I didn't know what was going on here. So this really isn't the Department of Social Harmony?

PORK: (*In a thundering voice.*) What's all this dinking, dinkety-dink Department stuff! We're not here to play tiddlywinks! You were told from the start!

ALEXANDRO: And you over there, who are you? Señores Stockholders, Sandwich-men, Policemen? Who are you?

ATTENDANTS: We're the actual executioners.

PORK: Finish him off!

MARIA: Don't you dare! Don't you touch him! He's my sweetheart!

PORK: Finish the game!

(*One of the* Attendants *switches the current on* Alexandro. Alexandro *falls out of the chair to the floor.* Pork *goes out rubbing his hands.* Feodoro *makes a cross in his ledger and goes out too. The* Attendants *carry* Alexandro*'s body to the proscenium and go out also. Only* Maria *remains. She runs to the proscenium and kneels beside* Alexandro*'s body.*)

MARIA: Are you dead, my dearest?

ALEXANDRO: Seems so.

MARIA: Maybe you really aren't dead yet? Maybe you're only in a deep coma?

ALEXANDRO: I don't know. I haven't figured it out yet. Where are all the people, where are all those fictional characters? If they have stopped existing, it means that I'm dead.

MARIA: (*Jumping up, yells.*) Hey, where are you all? Come on out!

(*At the rear of the stage there appear:* Feodoro, Gregoro, Miquelo, *the* Stockholders, *the* Man of Independent Means, *the* Playboy, *the* Bacchantes, *the* Blue- and-White-Collar Workers, Lola, Bobo, Chiquito.)

MARIA: (*Runs from one to the other.*) Join hands now, stretch out your arms, form a shapely narrative line. My sweetheart wants to see you all here.

CHARACTERS: (*Joining hands and singing softly.*)

> Our nice little Alexandro,
> Poor, poor little Alexandro,
> Beautiful Alexandro,
> Where did you fly away to?

MARIA: Sweetheart, you see, they're all here! Think up a happy ending!

ALEXANDRO: I'd think up a happy ending if I wasn't dead.

(Pork Sausage *runs across the stage with a bottle under his arm.*)

PORK: Drink Masculinus whisky! (*Disappears.*)

(*The Characters dissolve into the darkness one after the other.*)

MARIA: Where are you going? Don't leave! Hey!

(*On stage, total darkness and emptiness.* Maria *slowly approaches* Alexandro*'s body and sits down beside it.*)

MARIA: Now you're quite dead, aren't you, my dearest?
ALEXANDRO: Yes, my darling, I'm quite dead.
MARIA: What are you dreaming about?
ALEXANDRO: The same thing as always. About the island, about ourselves, with our friends, and about creating the true and the beautiful …
MARIA: And who knows, maybe we are there? Maybe we've always been there? Maybe we never were here at all?
ALEXANDRO: Maybe, who knows …

(*All the lights go out.*)

Curtain

SCENE EIGHT

The same setting as in the Prologue: an island, a palm tree. On stage Pork Sausage's *enormous head.* Maria, Gregoro *and* Miquelo *stand in a row. A bit removed to one side,* Alexandro *stands dumbfounded.*

HEAD: Form two columns!

(*After some confusion, the enlisted personnel form two columns.*)

HEAD: Forward, march!
ENLISTED PERSONNEL: (*Marching.*)

Masculinus, Masculinus!
Won't you cheer us!
Won't you cheer us!

ALEXANDRO: (*Yelling joyfully.*) Stop, boys! Look, a head round as a ball! Miquelo, to you!

(*Kicks the* Head *with his foot like a soccer ball.*)

MIQUELO: (*Joyfully.*) Got it! Gregoro, I'm going to shoot it on ahead! (*Sends the* Head *forward.*)
GREGORO: (*Runs after the* Head.) To you, Alexandro! (*Kicks it.*)
MARIA: (*Jumping up.*) What about me? What about me? Shoot it to me!
ALEXANDRO: To you, Maria!

(*A joyous game starts. All four of them run after the* Head, *yelling and pushing one another.*)

HEAD: (*Reverberating, with a groan.*) Not so hard, not so hard, to hell with you, you idiots!

(*With a powerful kick* Alexandro *knocks the* Head *offstage.*)

MARIA: It drowned! Too bad! We could have played volley-ball!
MIQUELO: You couldn't play much on an empty stomach, anyhow.
GREGORO: Yes, that's right. My legs are giving way I'm so weak.
ALEXANDRO: Attention! (*Goes over to the palm tree.*) Oh, Freedom Tree, send us something! (*Shakes the palm tree.*)

(*Many, many multicolored parachutes bearing packages slowly descend from above.*)

MIQUELO: Good gracious! Ham! Bologna! Hot dogs!
GREGORO: Cheeses! Roquefort! Camembert!
MARIA: Candies! Chocolate truffles! Layer cakes!

(*Two lovely bathing beauties descend from above on parachutes.*)

MIQUELO: My sweetheart has come! Rosita!
GREGORO: My Marquetta!
MARIA: My girlfriends! Rosita! Marquetta!

(*And finally another parachute comes down from above bearing a huge dark bottle with its neck wrapped in silverfoil.*)

ALEXANDRO: Hurrah, friends! Soviet champagne!

THE END

VASSILY AKSYONOV

Vassily Pavlovich Aksyonov was born on August 20, 1932 in Kazan in the former Soviet Union. His parents, both Communist party officials, were arrested during the Terror in the mid-1930s and sent to the gulags; they were freed and rehabilitated only after Stalin's death. His mother, Evgenia Ginzburg, told the story of her imprisonment in two celebrated and frequently dramatized memoirs: *Journey Into the Whirlwind* and *Within the Whirlwind*.

Vassily was taken in by relatives and raised in a state home for children of enemies of the people. He graduated from the Leningrad Medical Institute in 1956 and worked as a seaport quarantine doctor and then as a general practitioner in the Far North before specializing in tuberculosis. At the same time he started writing fiction, and with the publication of his novella *Colleagues* in 1960 in the magazine, *Yunost' (Youth)*, he became the leader of the post-war generation of young Russian artists. Abandoning his career as a doctor for that of a writer, Aksyonov published a series of novels – *A Ticket to the Stars, Halfway to the Moon*, and *Oranges from Morocco* – that portrayed the disaffected Soviet youth of the 1960s, attracted to Western pop culture and yet still marked by the collective dream of a better society.

His first work for the stage, *Always on Sale*, was directed by Oleg Yefremov at the Sovremennik (Contemporary) Theatre in 1966, but all his subsequent plays were forbidden by the censor and could be neither performed nor published. *Your Murderer* deals with "the eternal theme of the artist and power." As the author explains, "The play was written under the influence of the ideas expounded at the historic meeting of the Party and Government leaders with representatives of the creative intelligentsia in March 1963 in the Kremlin." In his richly allusive parable, Aksyonov shows the complicity of artists in the totalitarian project of imposing a new reality. The writers and artists in *Your Murderer* succumb to the temptation to wield political power to shape the world.

Despite his difficulties with the authorities, Aksyonov continued writing stories and novels, such as *The Island of Crimea* (1981), which were complex blends of satire, fantasy, and parody, written in a highly inventive style. He taught at UCLA on a visit to the United States in 1975 and wrote a novel about his experiences in California, called *24 Hours*.

Constantly at odds with the authorities, Vassily became one of the principal editors of the literary almanac *Metropol,* which set out to be an autonomous, uncensored periodical that would publish material rejected elsewhere. The homemade edition of only twelve copies of *Metropol* was reviled by the government as anti-Soviet propaganda. In 1979 Aksyonov resigned from the Writer's Union when two young applicants who had contributed to the almanac were refused membership, and in 1980 he was forced into exile, coming to America where he became Writer-in-Residence at Goucher College, Maryland. He has continued producing novels, among them *The Burn* (1980), about five Russian intellectuals, *In Search of Melancholy Baby* (1987), dealing with his travels across America, and *Generations of Winter,* a historical novel about a Russian family from 1925 to 1945. In 1990 Aksyonov's citizenship was restored, and he is now recognized as a major figure in Russian literature of the late twentieth century.

Other titles in the Russian Theatre Archive series:

Volume 12
Moscow Performances
The New Russian Theater 1991–1996
John Freedman

Volume 13
Lyric Incarnate
The Dramas of Aleksandr Blok
Timothy C. Westphalen

Volume 14
Russian Mirror: Three Plays by Russian Women
edited by Melissa Smith

Volume 15
Two Comedies by Catherine the Great, Empress of Russia:
Oh, These Times! and *The Siberian Shaman*
translated and edited by Lurana Donnels O'Malley

Volume 16
Off Nevsky Prospect:
St Petersburg's Theatre Studios in the 1980s and 1990s
Elena Markova

Volume 17
Stanislavsky in Focus
Sharon Marie Carnicke

Volume 18
Two Plays by Olga Mukhina
translated and edited by John Freedman

Volume 19
The Simpleton
by Sergei Kokovkin
translated and edited by John Freedman

Volume 20
Moscow Performances II
The 1996–1997 Season
John Freedman

Volume 21
Your Murderer
by Vassily Aksyonov
translated by Daniel Gerould and Jadwiga Kosicka, with an introduction by Daniel Gerould

This book is part of a series. The publisher will accept continuation orders which may be cancelled at any time and which provide for automatic billing and shipping of each title in the series upon publication. Please write for details.